HIGH PRAISE FOR THE WORKS OF
WAYNE C. LEE

"Lee's commanding grasp of history is combined with a colorful storytelling."
—*Midwest Book Review* on *Bad Men & Bad Towns*

"Trails of the Smoky Hill is a rip-roaring account of the Old West."
—*The Neshoba Democrat*

"An excellent example of what can be done with a vast amount of material...A worthwhile study for the beginning history buff."
—*True West Magazine* on *Deadly Days in Kansas*

ONLY ONE WILL LIVE

Web knew that he'd never ride away from Tree alive unless he left Rakaw dead behind him.

"I asked you a question," Rakaw said. "What did you find out?"

"Enough," Web said. "What are you going to do about it?"

Web didn't exaggerate his chances. Rakaw was a gunman; Web hadn't tried for speed from his gun for a long time. But there was only one way out of that yard for either of them now. That was past the dead body of the other.

Other *Leisure* books by Wayne C. Lee:

BLOOD ON THE PRAIRIE

THE HOSTILE LAND

Wayne C. Lee

LEISURE BOOKS NEW YORK CITY

A LEISURE BOOK®

February 2009

Published by special arrangement with Golden West Literary Agency.

Dorchester Publishing Co., Inc.
200 Madison Avenue
New York, NY 10016

ISBN 10: 0-8439-6170-8
ISBN 13: 978-0-8439-6170-6

Visit us on the web at www.dorchesterpub.com.

THE HOSTILE LAND

Wayne C. Lee

LEISURE BOOKS NEW YORK CITY

A LEISURE BOOK®

February 2009

Published by special arrangement with Golden West Literary Agency.

Dorchester Publishing Co., Inc.
200 Madison Avenue
New York, NY 10016

ISBN 10: 0-8439-6170-8
ISBN 13: 978-0-8439-6170-6

Visit us on the web at www.dorchesterpub.com.

tridges into the chambers and stuck more into the loops in the belt. Two minutes later he led his horse out of the barn and mounted him, heading east, crossing Dutchman Creek at an angle and pointing his horse toward his nearest neighbor.

Riding into the neighbor's yard, he dismounted as Gil Harris came out of the little house. It was a small frame house, one of the few homesteads along the Dutchman that could boast of anything but a soddy. Web was glad that his sister, Becky, had a nicer house than most.

"Ready, Gil?" Web asked of his brother-in-law.

"I guess." There wasn't much enthusiasm in Gil Harris' voice.

Web wondered, as he had so often, if he had been right in persuading Gil to take the homestead the day Gil and Becky were married four years ago. It had seemed the right thing to do then. But Gil just wasn't cut from the right cloth to make a dirt farmer or even a shirt-tail rancher.

Web said nothing about the warning shot as Gil got his horse and they rode silently out of the yard, heading east toward John Niccum's homestead half a mile away.

"How many do you think will be there?" Gil

Harris asked when the light from the window of his house dropped behind a knoll.

"All the homesteaders within ten miles, I hope," Web said. "You know what's happening. If we don't stick together, none of us will survive."

"Nobody can blame the fellows up on the dry land if they pull stakes," Harris said. "Only the lucky few of us who have land along the creek can stick it out if we don't get rain right away."

"We can stick together; help each other," Web said. "If we don't, Tree will gobble up all those homesteaders on the dry land. Then those of us on the creek will be surrounded, and we'll be squeezed to death."

"Are you really going to fight your own father?"

"It's his choice," Web said grimly. "I tried to get him to fight these homesteaders when they first started showing up in this country, but he wouldn't. Now he's fighting, but I'm on the other side."

Web recalled the events that had brought about this situation. He had discovered that Eli had no claim on two choice quarters on the creek next to Tree and had been bribing the locator not

THE HOSTILE LAND

I

Web Blaine wore no gun when he stepped outside his soddy just at sundown. He hadn't worn a gun in four years, not since he had left Eli Blaine's Tree Ranch and taken this homestead.

But he hadn't moved a foot from his door before he wished he had a gun in his hand now. The spang of a rifle echoed across the valley, and a bullet ripped wood from a rafter protruding from under the eaves. The bullet had hit a full two feet from his head, but Web dropped flat on his face and rolled back into the deep doorway of the soddy.

Up on the slope two hundred yards to the west, a man leaped on a horse and spurred him over the ridge out of sight. Web, looking directly into the sun, could only guess who the man was.

He got up slowly and dusted himself off. Somebody had heard about the meeting tonight, somebody who wasn't supposed to know. That shot had been just a warning. For no man intent on killing would have missed such an easy target by such a big margin.

He glanced up at the splintered rafter. If it had been a printed letter, he wouldn't have been able to read the message any clearer. But he wouldn't turn back now. He had called the meeting tonight at John Niccum's homestead, and he'd be there to present the facts. The bullet that changed his mind would have to come a lot closer than a rafter two feet from his head. For if he failed tonight, he might as well close the door of his soddy and walk away from four years of work.

He took a step toward his little barn to get his horse, then stopped and wheeled back into the house. Along the far wall of the bedroom of the two-room soddy was a trunk. He jerked up the lid and pulled out a gun belt that had been folded neatly among the clothes. Buckling the belt around his waist, he lifted the .45 from the holster and spun the cylinder. Even though he hadn't used the gun for four years, he had kept it well oiled and in perfect condition.

Digging deeper into the trunk, he brought up a box of ammunition, then punched five carto show them. When he was twenty-one, Web had filed on one of the quarters and had persuaded Gil Harris to take the other so they could keep all the land in the family. But Eli had been enraged. He said they had stolen the land from him and he had ordered them off Tree. Now he was determined to run Web off his homestead. Web's jaw hardened. Maybe he was just as stubborn as Eli.

"Eli Blaine isn't the only one buying up these homesteads," Gil Harris said.

"Who else?" Web demanded.

"Henry Farnsworth has made a standing offer to any settler who wants to get out of the country with a whole hide. A hundred dollars cash for the title to his land. Farnsworth then pays the government what's still due, if anything is, and he has clear title to a hundred and sixty acres of land."

"Many takers?"

"Several, I hear," Harris said. "Most of the homesteaders figure they're licked and are going to lose everything. If they can get out of the country with a hundred dollars, they're lucky."

The road they were following cut south along the edge of a plowed field where crops should have been, but now only the parched earth lay dark under the night sky. John Niccum didn't have a choice piece of land. Dutchman Creek cut across only the southwestern tip of his land. The rest of the ground was up off the flats, where it depended on rain for life-giving moisture. And the rains hadn't come for a long time.

"We should have held the meeting in town," Gil Harris grumbled as they approached Niccum's soddy. "A sod shack like that is no place to call the homesteaders together if you're going to try to convince them this is a wonderful country where everybody gets rich and happy."

"Nobody will try to tell them they're going to get rich overnight," Web said. "Besides, town is no place to hold a meeting like this. Tree might have some riders in town tonight. And if Farnsworth is buying out settlers, he certainly wouldn't like what we're going to try to do."

A lantern was hanging on a post outside John Niccum's door. Six saddle horses and two spring wagons were already in the yard. Web and Gil Harris dismounted, tied their horses and went inside.

"About time you showed up," Billy McNeil said to Web when he stepped into the room where the men waited.

Billy was a small man, the smallest man in the room. He was a couple of years older than Web and, like Web, was unmarried. His homestead was on the creek, too, just on the other side of Tree. There was a bond between them that had started growing the first time they had seen each other, and they had needed nothing more in common than just being neighbors to make them fast friends.

"What's this meeting for, Web?" a six-and-a-half-foot giant of a man demanded.

Web looked at Ed Ekhart, who owned the homestead directly south of John Niccum. "To keep everybody from running scared, if we can," he said.

Then his eyes traveled on over the group. There was Otto Blessing, whose homestead was directly north of Web's and Todd Martin, whose land was just east of Blessing's. There were other men from farther north up on the hard flat land that had yielded so fruitfully the first few years they had been there and now was so dry and barren.

Then there was Ivan Sitzman, a blond blue-eyed stump of a man who weighed as much as

Web but was half a foot shorter. His homestead was on the Dutchman, too, joining Billy Mc-Neil's on the west. He would stick with any group that fought to hold the land, Web thought. He had good land and the stubborn tenacity of a bulldog.

Web found a corner of the room where he could face everyone and looked at the expectant faces. Some were eager; some were doubtful; all were curious.

"Will there be fighting?" one man asked. "With guns, I mean."

"This is a civilized country now," Web said, choosing his words carefully. "Gun fights belong to the days of the cattle trails up from Texas. Those days are gone. But we do face a fight, all right, a fight to save our homes. The drought has hit us all, some harder than others. But it will rain again."

"When?" came a disgusted voice.

"You don't have to think back more than three or four years to bumper crops. If the land produced like that once, it will do it again. It takes a little vision and determination to stick by a thing through both the ups and downs."

"Takes a little grub, too," Otto Blessing said.

"My kids are hungry."

"Will they be any better fed if you take them some place where you don't even have a job and nothing you can call your own?" Web said. "Here you have a roof over their heads, and it's all your own. When the rains come again and you raise your crops, those crops will be all yours, too; not just the renter's share."

"What do you suggest we do till the rains come?" Todd Martin demanded.

"The proposition I have is this," Web said. "We pool our resources and help those who need it till we can raise a crop. If we don't, the big ranchers will take over this country again. And they'll never let the farmer in again once they get him out. You know as well as I do that the land north of the creek is farm land. A lot of you have your homes here. You can't just walk out and let everything you've worked for be trampled down by cattle."

"Who's got enough to share with anybody else?" Gil Harris asked.

"Yeah!" echoed a small man whose homestead north of the creek had never been well farmed. "All you want is for us suckers to stay and fight for this land so you won't lose your place to your old man."

A murmur of agreement ran through the room. Web had expected that when he had spied Newt Prandell in the crowd. Prandell was a poor excuse of a farmer. Even in prosperous years, his homestead had been a laughingstock of the country. Web didn't understand how he had managed to hang on this long. And he was a troublemaker wherever he went.

"It's for everybody's good," Web said. "It's your own homes you're trying to save. If we don't stick together, none of us will survive."

"I'm with you," Ivan Sitzman said in a booming voice. "They won't run me off my place. And if the rest of you have any backbone, they won't run you out, either."

Web ran his eyes over the men as they discussed things among themselves. He could pick the men he could depend on to stick with him: Ivan Sitzman, Billy McNeil, Ed Ekhart and John Niccum. All had homesteads on the creek or near it. Gil Harris had one of the choice quarters, too, but Web wasn't at all sure he could depend on his brother-in-law to put up much resistance if the pressure got heavy. Web's neighbors to the north, Otto Blessing and Todd Martin, seemed to be

siding with those who thought it wise to take what
they could get out of their farms and sneak out
of the country with whole hides and full bellies.

Web started to call for attention again when
a window just behind him shattered, showering
glass over the men in the room. Web hit the floor
as the crack of a rifle echoed in the yard outside.

Web didn't stir for a minute, listening for another shot which didn't come. John Niccum had
one of the few soddies in the country that had
glass windows. Most just had holes in the wall
with wooden shutters that fitted into the holes in
winter and during summer storms.

The sound of a running horse came from the
yard. Web got to his feet and dashed to the door,
jerking it open. A rider was just disappearing
into the night.

"I guess that answers your question about
whether there will be gun fighting, Newt," Otto
Blessing said in the stillness as the men considered the shot in stunned disbelief.

"They're trying to run a bluff," Web said
quickly. "Gun law is a thing of the past."

"That rifle shot didn't sound like it came out of
the past," Todd Martin said. "I'd guess it came

from Tree. How about you fellows?"

Several assenting voices rose in agreement. But Ed Ekhart shook his head.

"We're closer to town than we are to Tree," he said. "I'd guess Farnsworth was behind that shot."

"Farnsworth is a big fat toad," one man said. "He wouldn't ride out here for anything less than to kill a man. And that shot wasn't aimed at anybody."

"I'm glad you see that it wasn't intended to hurt anyone," Web said. "It was a bluff, nothing more."

"Maybe it was Farnsworth's gunhand, Jube Altson," Otto Blessing said. "And don't tell me he wouldn't shoot a man if he was paid enough to do it."

Web saw that the effectiveness of the meeting had been lost. Regardless of where the gunman had come from, he had accomplished his purpose. Then the strident voice of Newt Prandell cut through the bable of sound.

"I've been here as long as anybody," he shouted. "I know Eli Blaine. I say it was one of his men who fired that shot. I'd bet my life on it."

Anger rose in Web. He was a long way from

seeing eye to eye with his father; in fact, he knew he was facing a bitter fight with Eli. But he would never believe that his father would stoop to firing a shot through a man's window to scare him.

"You might bet your life on that and lose the bet, Prandell," Web said hotly.

"Hold on, Web," Billy McNeil said quickly at Web's elbow. "Prandell may have a point. I agree that Eli Blaine himself wouldn't fire a shot through a man's window. But he's got a foreman who might. And there are several new hands on Tree who look as if they'd love to do a job like this."

"Are you saying Eli doesn't control Tree any more?" Web demanded.

"You haven't been over to Tree for a while, have you, Web?" Billy asked.

"Not for a long while," Web said. "And I don't expect to be there soon, either."

"There are several new men there now," Billy said. "Tough men, the kind you wouldn't turn your back to."

"It was just a warning shot," Ivan Sitzman bellowed. "I'm not going to let it bluff me out."

"That's right, Ivan," Web agreed. "They were only trying to scare us. And I won't scare."

"If I was Eli Blaine's son, I wouldn't scare, either," Newt Prandell shouted in his strident voice.

"What do you mean by that?" Web demanded angrily. "You don't think Eli Blaine would harm his own son, do you?"

If Billy McNeil hadn't laid a hand on Web's arm, there would have been a little homesteader from north of the creek with a broken nose. Web tried to quiet the seething fury inside him. He'd always had a bad temper. He was like his father in that.

"If there is one man Eli Blaine would like to get off his homestead," Web said through clenched teeth, "it's me. If he was going to start a war on homesteaders, he'd start on me, not you fellows. Sneaking around and shooting through windows is not Eli Blaine's way."

"Why don't you prove it?" Todd Martin said. "Go over to Tree and face the old lion. If he did it or ordered it done, he'll admit it."

Web nodded. "He would, all right. And I'll do just that. Now I'm not standing up for Tree. Eli Blaine will run us all out if we'll run. But if he does, there'll be nothing sneaky about the way he does it."

II

As Web left his little soddy the next morning, he looked again at the splintered rafter to remind him that it hadn't been just a bad dream. When he put his gun away four years ago he hadn't ever expected to wear it again and, though he wasn't wearing it this morning on his mission to Tree, he couldn't get rid of the feeling that he would wear it and use it again before this was settled.

Web hadn't been at Tree headquarters for two years. He had been across Tree land several times, and whenever he rode up the creek to Billy McNeil's homestead he crossed the land claimed by Sim Dalbow. That quarter joined Tree on the north, and Dalbow had filed homestead papers on it. He had built a tiny shack and spent at least one night there each six months, just enough to fulfill minimum requirements to obtain land by homestead. Eli Blaine had paid him to do it, Web knew, and Tree had absorbed the homestead once Dalbow had gained clear title to it.

When Web came in sight of the big white house and barn on Tree, he was swept by a wave of nostalgia as he always was when he looked at the ranch headquarters. For fifteen years, from the time he was six years old until he took the homestead, Tree had been his home. That big house and barn hadn't been there at the beginning. Both house and barn had been sod then, and the nearest neighbor had been more than fifteen miles away.

Along the creek bank was the orchard of apple and cherry trees that Web and his father had set out and tended so carefully. Those trees had grown and borne fruit in years when the late frosts hadn't killed the blossoms.

Web rode along the river trail until he was at the edge of the orchard, remembering the hours he had whiled away there, playing in the trees and in the creek nearby when he was supposed to be hoeing the weeds away from the trees.

Suddenly he reined up. Two men had appeared

from the trees, one on either side of him. One caught the bridle of his horse, commanding, "Hold it right there!"

The man was heavy-set, with red hair straggling down from under his hat and a red-blotched face with two front teeth pushing out from between thick lips. The other man was smaller by twenty-five or thirty pounds, with sandy hair and pale, almost colorless eyes.

Web didn't move; he just stared at the two men, wishing he had buckled on his gun that morning.

"Your horse is pointed the wrong way," the redheaded man said. "We don't want sodbusters fouling up the air around here."

"I've got business with Eli Blaine," Web said.

"I suppose you claim to be working here?"

"We draw our pay every month," the smaller man said. "I don't remember Eli saying he had invited any clodhoppers to visit him."

"I'm Web Blaine," Web said. "Now get out of the way."

"I'm Jess Rakaw, and my sidekick is Ray Hickman. Those names mean anything to you? Just because your name is Blaine don't make you look no different to us from any other sodbuster.

You've got just two choices. Turn this plug around and go home, or get off and try to walk over us to the house. Which is it going to be?"

Web considered trying to spur his horse over the sneering redhead. But Rakaw was standing too far to one side, apparently anticipating such a move. The smart thing would be turn around and go back as Rakaw suggested. But anger was boiling in Web now. He wasn't about to turn and run. That was what those rifle shots last night had been meant to do—make a man run.

Web eased his feet free of the stirrups while studying the two men. Bunching his muscles, he lunged off the horse straight at Hickman, who was closer than Rakaw.

He struck Hickman in the chest and stomach, driving the breath from him as they hit the ground and rolled over. Web jerked away from Hickman, who just rolled farther away and groaned, not making any effort to get up.

Rakaw had released the horse and was now lunging for Web. Web rolled away, bumping into a tree. Using the tree for a handhold, Web got to his feet just as Rakaw reached him.

Rakaw's fist grazed Web's jaw, and Web saw lights stabbing before his eyes. He backed quickly around the tree, shaking his head to clear it. Then Rakaw was around the tree, too, swinging a fist in a great arc. Web ducked and drove his own fist into the pit of Rakaw's stomach. Breath exploded from the redhead, but he only staggered back a step, then came on again.

Web met this charge with two quick fists in the face, bringing blood from a mashed nose. Rakaw bellowed in pain and rage and bored in again. One wild swing connected on Web's cheek bone, and he went down as if a tree had fallen on him.

Rakaw lunged at him, an animal hiss of triumph whistling through his thick lips. But Wade twisted to one side, and Rakaw hit the ground with a jarring crash. Web was on his feet before the slower Rakaw could get up. As Rakaw straightened, Web hit him across his wounded nose and one eye. As the redhead backed off, Web followed up with two more punches, either one powerful enough to fell an ordinary man. But Rakaw stayed on his feet.

The redhead was swinging wildly now, bellowing in helpless rage. Then his retreat was stopped against an apple tree. Before he could move away, Web hit him twice more, putting everything he could behind each blow. Rakaw, blood trickling from his mouth, pushed a curse through puffed lips; then his head sagged to one side, and his big body followed it.

As Rakaw slid to the foot of the tree, all fight gone from him, Web saw the other man getting to his feet, crouching, ready to spring at him. Wheeling, he faced the pale-eyed man, and Hickman stopped as if suddenly turned to stone. Web moved a step toward him, and Hickman lifted both hands, palms out.

"I'm out of it," he panted, still laboring for his breath.

"You wanted to play rough," Web said, still advancing.

Hickman backed away faster. "I'm out of it," he repeated. Then he turned and broke into a run toward the bunkhouse, just beyond the big house.

Web turned back slowly and looked at the slumped form of Rakaw. The redhead was stirring, mumbling incoherently. Web walked to his horse, which had wandered only a few yards away where some knee-high grass was growing close to the creek.

Mounting slowly, Web realized how many blows Rakaw had landed and how they had bruised. He reined his horse into the trail and urged him up to the hitchrack in front of the house, which stood on a little knoll, safely above the flood waters that sometimes swept down the Dutchman in the spring of the year.

Dismounting at the hitchrack, Web walked up to the house. He looked across at the bunkhouse, but Hickman wasn't in sight. Sim Dalbow, foreman on Tree for the last fifteen years, was lounging in front of the bunkhouse door, watching Web's every move with his slate-colored eyes. But he gave no sign of recognition, and Web returned his cold, impersonal stare.

Dalbow had come to Tree when Web was eight. He had come up the trail from Texas with a herd, he said, and he didn't want to go back. Eli had hired him and a couple of years later made him foreman of Tree. He still had that job. Web had never felt close to Dalbow, but he had never had occasion to lock horns with him, either. Dalbow was something of a loner, doing his job and doing it well. He had always been loyal to Eli Blaine.

Web walked into the house without knocking. He wanted to face Eli and get it over. But the living room was empty. He stood there a moment, wondering what his next move should be. His mother came from the kitchen. Her cry of surprise brought him whirling around. There was no mistaking the eager welcome in her voice.

"It's good to see you, Web."

"I came to see Eli," Web said. "There are some things going on that need explaining. I think maybe he can do it."

Mrs. Blaine sat down in a rocker, and Web dropped in a chair by the table. A worried frown touched Loretta Blaine's face.

"Bad things are in the wind, Web," she said. "But don't be too harsh in judging your father. He's had a hard life."

Web nodded. "I know. Now he's making it hard on everyone else."

"I've never told you much of what your father went through, Web. Maybe you ought to know now. If you understood some of the trials he's had, it might make you see his side of things better."

Web waited. He doubted if anything his mother could say would make him see things Eli's way. But he didn't want to do anything to hurt his mother more than she had already been hurt by the split in her family.

"Eli and I were married during the war, you

know," Loretta Blaine said. "He was from Pennsylvania, and I was born and raised in Memphis. Eli was with Serman's command and was in Memphis in '62. We were married secretly. Only my parents knew about it. Eli went on with his army unit, but when your older brother, William, was born, Eli's commander was notified. Not long after that Eli was accused of passing information to the Confederates. Eli thought he was suspected because his wife was a Southerner. The charge couldn't be proved, but it left a stain on Eli's reputation and made him an angry, bitter man.

"He was wounded in '64 and discharged. We moved to Pennsylvania near his old home. Walter was born there. Eli was in constant trouble. There were those who believed that he had betrayed his government and slipped information to the Confederates. Eli got into one fight after another. After the war, we left there and moved down to Tennessee, just a short distance from Memphis. But there they resented him because he was a Yankee and had fought for the Union. We stayed there four years. You were born there just before we left."

"He had fights there, too, I suppose," Web

said when his mother paused.

"All the time. Eli wouldn't take an insult without fighting. And he heard very little but insults. Shortly after you were born, we moved to Missouri. But somehow Eli's history and his reputation for being a hard man to get along with followed him. He had fights there, too.

"Becky was born in Missouri. We finally had to leave there in '73. By then Eli was ready to fight anybody who even mentioned anything that he could consider an insult. We moved to Iowa and hadn't been there three months before Eli was in trouble again. He was branded a trouble-maker, and our neighbors simply got together and told us we weren't welcome and that we had to move on. You weren't old enough to remember that, I'm sure."

"I remember how mad we all were when we had to move, especially William."

"You probably remember where we lived in eastern Nebraska. Eli talked constantly about how nobody was going to push us around any more. We'd fight. I tried to get him to stop such talk, especially around the older boys. But he seemed to live for nothing but to prove that nobody could push him around again. They tried, mainly, I think, because he acted so cantankerous. It finally came to a fight."

Loretta Blaine paused again, bitter memories seeming to crowd out the words. But Web remembered what she couldn't tell. Two neighbors had argued constantly with Eli until it had grown into open war. The neighbors had threatened Eli, and Eli had invited them to a fight. When they came to the Blaine farm, they came shooting. It was a stand-off until Web's older brothers, William and Walter, twelve and ten then, had found guns and rushed into the fight. They were impetuous and careless, and both were killed. Web would never forget that black day as long as he lived. He had been only six at the time, but it had made an indelible impression.

"After that fight, I told Eli I'd leave him if he ever fought again," Loretta Blaine said softly. "He promised he wouldn't. Losing William and Walter took all the fight and most of the life out of him. We came out here to the Dutchman, where we had no neighbors and didn't ever expect to have any. But they came. Eli stood by his promise. When the homesteaders began crowding us off our range, Eli pulled back into the hills south of the creek."

"I know about that," Web said. "That's where he and I had our first disagreement. I wanted to fight for what was ours. He wouldn't."

"You're a lot like Eli, Web. Same temper when you're crowded into a corner. I hope you never let it get the best of you."

"Why is Eli fighting now?" Web asked. "He wouldn't fight when he had me to help him."

"When you took that homestead and Becky married Gil Harris, it did something to Eli," Loretta said in a low voice. "He felt that he had failed once by fighting and once by not fighting. He swore that if he ever got the chance, he'd fight the devil himself if necessary to build Tree back to its original size. When drought struck the country and the homesteaders began leaving, Eli saw his chance to get the land he wanted and get it legally, and he took it."

"Now he's trying to surround the few of us left along the creek and starve us out," Web said bitterly. "I won't stand by and let him get away with that."

"I'm hoping you can look at the life Eli has had and understand him better, Web. He doesn't want to fight you. But I think he will if he must to build Tree up again."

Web crossed to his mother and laid a hand on her shoulder. "Maybe not. Maybe I can make him see my side of it."

Hoofbeats sounded in the yard, and Loretta Blaine caught Web's hand. "That's your father, Web. Hadn't you better go?"

"I came here to see him," Web said.

"Be careful. Don't rile him."

Web looked at his mother and nodded. "All right, Ma. I'll ride easy."

He went back to his chair by the table and waited.

Boots clumped across the porch; then Eli Blaine strode through the door, a tall man carrying his fifty-odd years on straight shoulders. His thick hair, always unruly, was streaked with gray now, and his hard blue eyes seemed to pop from his head a little more than usual as they searched the room for Web.

"Well, what's on your mind?" he demanded, staring at Web.

The tone of Eli's voice brought Web up out of his chair, a frown tugging at his forehead. "Somebody took a shot at me last night at my place and then put another bullet through the window at John Niccum's where the homesteaders were holding a meeting. I want to find out what you know about it."

Anger blazed in Eli's eyes. "Nothing! And you know it. I don't shoot through windows. If I'm going to shoot a man, I tell him about it. Then I make the shot count."

"I didn't figure you did the shooting," Web said. "But I thought you might know who did. Maybe some Tree hand."

"Tree doesn't do any sneak shooting, either!" Eli roared. "If that's all you've got to say, you'd better move along."

"It's not all," Web said. "Who's this Jess Rakaw and Ray Hickman?"

"They're new hands here," Eli said, much of the anger fading from his voice.

"They don't look like men you'd hire," Web said.

"They're good men," Eli said. "We need lots of men to handle Tree, the way it's growing."

Web saw a change come over Eli. He was suddenly an old man, no longer a belligerent war horse. Web had never seen him like this, not even when he had knuckled under to the incoming settlers and withdrawn into the hills. He looked old and beaten.

III

Web reined up in front of Henry Farnsworth's General Store and dismounted. If anybody from town had been responsible for that bullet through Niccum's window last night, it had to be Farnsworth. Gil Harris had said Farnsworth was buying up land from the discouraged homesteaders. And Henry Farnsworth was the big wheel in town.

But Web had other interests drawing him into the coolness of the store. Ever since the winter term of school had ended in Bell, Valaree Prescott, the schoolteacher, had been working for Farnsworth as bookkeeper. Web liked to think he was partly the reason Valaree had sought a job in Bell instead of going back to her home in Omaha.

The inside of the store seemed dark after the

glare of the blazing sun outside, and Web stood for a minute just inside the door until his eyes became accustomed to the shadowy interior.

He saw Henry Farnsworth sitting, as usual, in his rocking chair behind the counter. Most stores had room behind the counter only for a sales clerk. But Farnsworth had pushed the counter out from the wall far enough to allow room for his big rocker.

Someone at the meeting last night had called Farnsworth a big fat toad. Web, looking at him rocking contentedly now, couldn't argue with the description. He was only a little over five and a half feet tall, but he weighed well over two hundred pounds. His bald head was ringed with a fringe of brown hair, and his green eyes were set back in his bloated face like two poisonous lizards hiding in deep rock crevices.

Farnsworth fanned himself with his cream-colored hat and spread his fat face in a grin that Web supposed was meant to be friendly.

"She's at her books," he said softly.

Web merely nodded. Farnsworth had always appeared friendly to Web. But Web couldn't reconcile that friendliness with the chilled animosity he felt whenever he was near the fat man.

Farnsworth hated him, and Web didn't know why.

Web walked down the length of the counter to a little square space at the end where Valaree Prescott was bent over some books. Valaree was just a couple of years younger than Web. The contrast between her and her employer was startling. Web had seen Farnsworth and Valaree standing or walking together several times. They were almost exactly the same height. But Valaree was over a hundred pounds lighter. And her long blonde hair and sky blue eyes were in sharp contrast to Farnsworth's dark complexion.

She kept on working as Web approached.

"You're working too hard, Valaree," Web said, stopping at her elbow.

She laid down the pencil and looked up. "I had a column I wanted to get added right before I let it get out of my mind." She motioned to a chair next to the counter. "Sit down, Web. I haven't seen you lately."

"Been busy," he said. "How about you?"

"I've been busy, too, Web. Seems like I can't catch up."

"Shouldn't be that much book work in a little outfit like this store."

She shook her head. "You're wrong. There is plenty of work. Most of it is trying to untangle back accounts that haven't been kept up since Mr. Farnsworth opened his store."

"Anything unusual going on lately?" Web asked.

The little smile on Valaree's lips faded, and she pretended to think hard. Web watched her, suspicions nagging at him.

"I can't think of a thing unusual," Valaree said after a minute.

"Somebody put a rifle bullet through John Niccum's window last night," Web said. "Heard anything about that?"

She nodded. "I heard about it, all right. Ed Ekhart was in here this morning telling about it. He seemed to think it might have been Jube Altson who did it."

"He didn't say that, did he?"

"He did. You know Ed. He never minces around with words. He says exactly what he thought."

Web nodded.

"I hear Farnsworth is buying up some homesteads from fellows who are pulling out," Web said.

"Maybe," Valaree said vaguely. "You know a bookkeeper is a confidential employee. She can't tell what she finds in the books she works on."

Web didn't press the subject. He knew she would tell him if she wanted him to know. Evidently she didn't.

"I really came in to see if you'd go to the dance with me tonight," he said, trying to recapture some of the magic that had once drawn them together.

"You know I will," she said, and for an instant her smile was warm. Then it faded. "But I'll have to get to work now, or I won't be ready on time."

Web couldn't believe that there was enough book work in the store to keep Valaree that busy. But he didn't argue. After all, she was going with him tonight. He couldn't ask for anything more.

Just as Web was leaving the store, he met Jube Altson coming in. Altson was a big man, as tall as Web and a little heavier, and his jet black eyes and hair gave him the look of the Dark Avenger. Altson played on his appearance by wearing only dark clothes, topped by a black Stetson.

Web could feel Altson's eyes on him as he went down the street and turned in at the bank, less

than a block from the store. Fred Bell held mortgages on many of the homesteads, and Web had
to know how those farmers stood with the bank.
It would determine how hard Web could push
them to stick it out.

Fred Bell was a mild-mannered, gray-haired
little man whose stooped shoulders seemed to
bend beneath his sixty years. He didn't appear
happy to see Web.

"What can I do for you, Web?" he asked like
a man asking when his hanging is to be.

"I'm not looking for a loan, if that's what's
worrying you, Web said.

Bell grinned feebly. "I guess it was. I've simply reached the point where I can't loan any more
money to these settlers. Too many are pulling
out, leaving me holding the bag. The country is
folding. It's not a good risk any more."

"You know that isn't so," Web said quickly.
"This is good farm land. Just because it's drying
out this year doesn't mean it won't come back.
Aren't you gambler enough to take a chance on
these men making a go of it? You'll be an important man and have a thriving bank once they
get on their feet again."

"All you're saying are words, Web. Look at

the facts. The farmers are licked. They can't survive without crops. And nobody can raise anything but a dust in this country. Short crop last year; absolutely nothing this year. They're pulling out of this place like it had the plague, and I don't blame them. Every time one of them leaves without paying off his loan, it makes the bank that much shakier. If you're leading up to asking for loans for more of the homesteaders, I'll tell you right now, the answer is no."

Web sighed heavily. He'd been afraid that was how it would be. He'd have to use some strong persuasion now to get the settlers to stick to their claims.

The door of the bank suddenly swung open, and Darlene Bell came in, almost on a run. Web had known Darlene since she was in pigtails. He had never guessed then that she'd fill out into the brown-eyed beauty she was now at twenty.

"Todd Martin is leaving," she announced dramatically.

Web saw Fred Bell's shoulders sag a little more. "That leaves the bank holding another mortgage," he said wearily.

"If he can't pay off his mortgage, you'll have his farm," Web said, fighting the despair he felt.

"What good is that?" Bell said. "The bank needs money. And that land is a poor substitute for money now."

"How come he's leaving?" Web asked Darlene. "I saw him last night. He didn't say anything then about leaving."

"He was beaten up last night on his way home from John Niccum's," Darlene said. "I didn't hear the details. He's in Farnsworth's now buying enough supplies to last him and his family till they can get some place where he can find a job."

Web sighed and turned back to look at Bell. "Guess you've got another farm whether you want it or not."

"I doubt that I'll even get that," Bell said. "There'll be Tree cattle on that place before the sun goes down."

"Tree?" Web exclaimed. "Tree doesn't own that."

"You tell that to Tree's foreman, Dalbow. I don't want to."

Anger boiled inside Web. "I may do just that—if he tries to put cattle on Martin's place."

Web whirled toward the door. There was something here that he didn't understand. Todd Martin should have some answers, and Web was going to hear them before Martin left town.

He strode up the street toward the store. But before he got there, he saw Todd Martin come out of the store, carrying a gunny sack filled with supplies. His wife and two children were in the wagon, Mrs. Martin sitting on the big seat, staring stolidly straight ahead.

Martin had climbed up to the seat and had unwrapped the reins from the brake handle when Web got to the wagon.

"Hold it a minute, Todd," Web said. "Darlene says you were beaten up last night. Who did it?"

"I don't know," Martin said. "There were three of them. One roped me off my horse; then they all jumped on me. Some of the land company men, I reckon."

"What land company?" Web asked in surprise.

"The Bell County Land Company," Martin said. "They tried to buy me out a week ago for a hundred dollars. I was a fool not to take it. Now I get nothing."

"Who is this land company?"

"I don't know that, either. The only men I've seen have been their tough hands. Jess Rakaw leads the pack."

"Tree!" Web exclaimed. "But why does Tree call itself a land company? And where would Eli get the money, even a hundred dollars, to offer to buy out settlers?"

"You're doing the asking," Martin said. "You can do the answering, too. I'm getting out of this dried up desert."

"Why did they pick on you?" Web asked, more to himself than to Martin.

"They pick on one at a time. Your turn will come. If you've got the sense you were born with, you'll make up with your old man and grow big with Tree. If you don't, you'll get run out or run over same as all the rest of us homesteaders."

Martin clucked to his team, and the loaded wagon creaked slowly down the street and turned southeast along the river road.

Web stood silently watching the wagon disappear behind the livery barn.

IV

The sun was barely up the next morning when the low bawling of cattle jerked Web away from his breakfast table. Those cattle were being driven. He'd been on too many drives himself not to recognize the low complaining bawl of cattle being pushed faster and farther than they wanted to go.

Outside his soddy, he turned toward the sound and saw the cattle moving along his northern boundary. They were partly on his land and partly on Otto Blessing's land. But Web knew where they were being driven. Fred Bell had said yesterday that Tree would have cattle on Todd Martin's land before anybody could do anything about it.

Web ran back into the house, anger rising in him like a fountain. Somebody would do something about it! He buckled on his gun belt and ran out to his barn to saddle his horse. Before the cattle reached Martin's homestead, which cornered Web's on the northeast, Web was in the saddle, urging his horse after the herd.

As he came close, he saw that there weren't many cattle; just enough to lay claim to Martin's quarter-section of land and destroy anything there there that might make the land look like an inhabited homestead.

There were only two riders with the cattle, and Web recognized Jess Rakaw and Ray Hickman. He had tangled with them yesterday morning in the orchard on Tree. It looked as if he was going to tangle with them again on Martin's homestead. Only this time it would be different. Neither Rakaw nor Hickman nor Web would climb off his horse to fight it out with fists this morning.

Web loosened the gun in his holster as he approached the cattle. He was almost to the herd when Rakaw spotted him. Rakaw yelled at Hickman, then wheeled away from the cattle and rode to meet Web.

"You're trespassing on Tree land," Rakow shouted.

"Who says so?" Web countered. "This land

belongs to the bank now that Martin's gone."

"Not any more, it doesn't," Rakaw said smugly.

Web considered Rakaw for a moment. The man seemed supremely confident.

"You'd better get those cattle out of here," Web said.

"You figure on running them off Tree land?" Rakaw asked, his eyes flashing in anticipation. "Just try it."

"Maybe I will," Web said.

It was going to have to come to a showdown between him and Rakaw some day. He'd only met the man yesterday morning, but they had clashed three times already.

But before the tension reached the breaking point, a shout from Web's left jerked him around. Sim Dalbow was racing toward them across a corner of Web's place.

Web waited, his attention still riveted on Rakaw. Chances were that Rakaw would do nothing now until Dalbow got there. But Web was taking no chances on the man. He wouldn't trust him any farther than he would an irritated bumblebee.

"What are you two roosters up to now?" Dalbow demanded, sliding his horse to a stop.

"This hairpin is trying to run our cattle off Tree land," Rakaw said, emphasizing the ownership of the land.

"I say he's crazier than a locoed horse, saying this land belongs to Tree," Web said, wondering why he should explain anything to Dalbow.

"Jess is right," Dalbow said. "Tree does own this land now."

"You're a liar," Web said. "The bank just took it over yesterday."

"Don't call me a liar!" Dalbow snapped. "Either back that up or go on to the bank and find out for yourself. Tree bought the mortgage from Fred Bell yesterday."

Web stared at the Tree foreman for a moment. "I'll check with Bell," he said. "Why would he sell the mortgage to Tree?"

"Ask him," Dalbow said easily. "Meanwhile, I'll thank you to leave these cattle alone."

Web fought against the feeling that he was licked. Dalbow was too sure of himself, too anxious for Web to talk to the banker. Well, he would talk to Fred Bell. There had to be an explanation for this.

He wheeled his horse around and pointed him

toward town. Anger built up in him as he rode.
Was Fred Bell in the land company, too? Web
wasn't certain how far the tentacles of the octopus
reached. Tree evidently was the center. Web had
reason to believe that Farnsworth was one arm
of the octopus. Was Fred Bell another? If so,
there wasn't much anybody in the valley could
do. Even the organization that Web was trying to
form among the homesteaders couldn't survive
against such a combination of power.

In town, Wade rode directly to the bank and
dismounted. The bank wasn't open yet, and he
had to wait until Fred Bell came down the street
and unlocked the door. Web followed him inside.

"Something on your mind, Web?" Bell asked.

"You know there is," Web said. "Sim Dalbow
tells me that Tree owns Todd Martin's place. Is
that right?"

The banker went into his office and dropped in
the chair behind his desk. "Not exactly. Todd
Martin is the legal owner until foreclosure pro-
ceedings are complete."

"But you own the note. You're the only one
who can foreclose."

Bell shrugged. "I don't own the note now. I
sold the note to the Bell County Land Company

last night. They'll have to foreclose. But you know that Martin won't fight it. You heard him say he was getting out and staying."

Webb nodded. "I heard. Why did you sell to the company? Are you part of it?"

"No," Bell said with convincing force. "But the bank can't absorb all these bad debts. I have to realize cash out of these loans. I'm taking a loss any way I look at it. But it's better for me to get something out of them than to be stuck with a lot of worthless land."

Web leaned across the desk. "You've got better foresight than that, Fred. You know that land is worth more than the company is paying you for those notes."

"Maybe," Bell said with a heavy sigh. "But the truth of it is, I spread myself too thin to make these loans. Now I've got to have cash to meet any withdrawal. There are certain depositors who could wreck the bank if they withdrew their money in a lump."

"Henry Farnsworth?" Web guessed.

"He's not exactly a poor man," Bell said.

Web nodded. "And if he jerked all his money out of your bank, you'd be in trouble. But as long as you go along with what he says, he'll leave his money here and you'll stay in business. Is that it?"

Web didn't wait for Bell to answer. It was obvious from the look of defeat on Bell's face that Web had guessed right. When Fred Bell was left with a mortgage the land company wanted, the company simply bought it, then foreclosed. Bell didn't dare refuse to sell.

If it was Farnsworth's threat to withdraw his money that made Bell jump to the tune played by the land company, then the fat storekeeper was the money power of the company. Yet it was Tree that moved in on the land as soon as the land company got it. That had to mean that Farnsworth and Tree were in it together.

Web strode out of the bank, his anger hotter than when he had come in. He didn't believe that Fred Bell was a real part of the land company, but he was contributing to its successful land grab as surely as if he were a member in good standing.

V

Two days later Web saw a rider coming toward his place from the north. It was noon, and the heat was enough to fry the life out of a man. Web had gone to the house to get a drink before returning to his work of repairing the fence around his corral.

Web put the dipper back in the bucket and stepped out where he could get a better view of the man riding toward him. He recognized Billy McNeil, and some of the tension drained out of him.

Billy reined up by the barn and dismounted, leading his horse into the barn.

"Looks like you've been pushing him," Web said, stepping into the barn doorway.

"Doesn't take much pushing to fag a horse in this heat," Billy said. He tied the reins, loosened the cinch and came outside. "Guess I was in a mite of a hurry, too. Ivan Sitzman just told me that Otto Blessing had sold out to the land company, and I came by to check on it."

Web frowned. "Did he?"

"He's not there, anyway. Everything's gone— wagon, chickens, cows, what little furniture he had. I reckon Ivan was right."

Web gripped the edge of the barn door until his fingers hurt. This was a body blow. Blessing's homestead bordered Web's on the north. If he had sold out to the company, that meant that Web's place was completely surrounded by the company's land except on the east where Gil Harris' homestead kept the road open to town.

"I suppose with Tree Ranch on one side and Martin's homestead overrun now with Tree cattle on the other, Otto figured he didn't have a chance of sticking it out," Web said.

"Puts you in a hot spot," Billy said. "You've just got one way out, through Gil's homestead. No telling—"

Billy stopped, but Web finished for him. "No telling when Gill will cave in under the pressure. You're right, Billy. If Gil quits, I'll be boxed in like a can of sardines. But I'm not quitting."

"I figured I had it bad enough," Billy said, "having Tree between me and town. But I've got a neighbor to the west who won't knuckle under, that's for sure. Ivan hates Tree like poison since Eli started grabbing land in every direction."

"We'll stick it out," Web said grimly. "If you run into any trouble, let me know. We'll have to stand together."

"You know you can depend on Ivan and me. Wish I could say that about some of the others."

After his horse had cooled off, Billy took him down to the creek for water then mounted and rode back across Tree range to his homestead.

Web went back to his work, making his corral tight enough to hold his few cows at night.

He had just finished eating supper, bone-weary and anticipating bed, when his attention was pulled to a glow in the southeastern sky. All thought of bed vanished as he looked. It was a fire, and it wasn't too far away. Quickly he made an estimate. It was in the direction of town, but it wasn't that far away. Ed Ekhart's place was on a direct line between Web's homestead and Bell.

Web quickly saddled his horse, buckled his gun around his waist and thundered out of the yard, heading east toward Gil Harris' place. He found Gil watching the fire but making no move to do anything about it.

"It's Ed's place," Web said, more certain than ever now that he got a line on the blaze from a new angle. "He'll need help."

"I can't leave my place," Harris said.

"You may have a point there," Web said. "But we have to stick together. If we each dig in and try to protect our own stuff whenever anything like this happens, they'll wipe us out one by one."

"I'll get my horse," Harris said. "Will you be all right, Becky?"

"Of course," Web's sister said. "They won't bother me. Anyway, I've got my rifle."

It seemed to Web that Gil Harris took a long time getting his horse saddled, but he finally led him from the barn, and they galloped to the southeast toward the blaze.

The glow began to die down before Web and Harris got to Ekhart's place. Web felt relief when he saw it was Ed's barn rather than the house that was burning. John Niccum was there helping Ekhart keep the blaze confined to the barn. All the wood in the building was being reduced to charred embers when Web and Harris reined up.

"What started it?" Web asked when he got to Ekhart.

"Don't know," Ekhart said. "They sure did a good job, though."

"You figure it was set?"

Ekhart looked at Web in surprise. "How else would a sod barn get on fire? The mangers, partitions, doors and roof are the only wood in it."

"Could have started in the hay," Web said.

"I reckon the hay made a good tinder to start the fire."

"Have any horses or cows in there?"

"I did have," Ekhart said. "Funny thing about that. Those critters were all loose and out of the barn when I came out to fight the fire."

Web frowned. "How did they get out?"

"Horses don't untie themselves from mangers," Ekhart said. "Somebody turned them out. At least they didn't want to burn the horses. I'll say that for them. I figure this is just a warning of worse things to come if I don't sell to the land company."

"You've had offers?"

"If you can call them that. A hundred dollars

for my place, and I pull out right now with what I own. Two hundred dollars, lock stock and barrel, and I just take my family. Now what kind of a price is that for a farm on river bottom land like I've got?"

"It's robbery," Web said. "Who made the offer?"

"The Tree foreman, Sim Dalbow. He was here twice. Pretty nasty the last time."

Web motioned to the barn, where only the sod walls now stood. "This is even nastier. What are you going to do?"

"I'm staying," Ekhart said. "I would have come nearer selling before they fired the barn than I would now. They may kill me, but I won't scare."

"If we could prove that they set that fire, it would bring the law in on our side," Web said thoughtfully.

"How can you do that? I know it and you know it. But neither one of us can prove it. Probably can't get the sheriff to ride all the way over here, anyway."

"I may try it," Web said. "Looks like the fire is about out now."

"John and I can keep it from spreading any

more," Ekhart said. "I don't think there was a thing you could have done if you'd been here when it started. My guess is that they threw coal oil over the hay and wood inside. It went up like an explosion."

Web nodded. "I'll ride to the county seat tomorrow and talk to the sheriff, anyway. It might do some good."

The next morning he left his place early to ride to the county seat and talk to the sheriff there. He didn't expect much in the way of results, but he had to try.

The sheriff was a middle-aged, mild-mannered man who looked as if he would rather stay in the cool shade of his office than try to see that justice was done, if it meant any exertion on his part.

"That's a long way to ride just to look at a heap of ashes," he said. "What makes you think somebody set that fire?"

"It was meant as a warning of worse things to come if Ekhart doesn't sell out."

"Maybe he should sell," the sheriff said, not making a move to get out of his chair.

"Would you just sit there if somebody set your jail on fire?"

The sheriff leaned forward. "Don't get any

fancy ideas, young fellow."

Web stared straight back at the officer. "That barn was just as important to Ed Ekhart as your jail is to you."

"All right." The sheriff got out of his chair. "You sure are a persistent booger. I'll ride out and look. But you know what chance I have of even proving it was arson, much less catching the fellow who touched it off."

Web nodded, some of his anger draining away. "I know. But just the fact that the sheriff came out to investigate might make them think twice before they tried anything else. They think they run that end of the county."

"They come mighty near doing it," the sheriff grumbled as he left the office. "Too big a territory for me to handle by myself."

Web followed the sheriff outside, feeling disgusted. It wasn't such a big country; it was just a case of a lazy or disinterested sheriff.

Before Web and the sheriff reached Bell, Web became convinced that the entire effort was wasted. It would be difficult for even a sharp eye to find anything around Ekhart's barn to prove that the fire had been deliberately set.

The sheriff followed the road into Bell instead

of angling off toward Ekhart's farm. Web didn't object. It wasn't far out of the way, and there was the chance that the sight of the sheriff in town might do some good, especially if certain people in town were even a little impressed by sight of the law.

The sheriff asked a few pointless questions that netted him nothing. Jube Altson lounged in front of Farnsworth's store and openly sneered at the sheriff, but the officer either didn't see or chose to ignore him.

At Ekhart's, the sheriff made a casual investigation and found nothing, just as Web had expected.

No fires blazed that night or the next. As time moved on and nothing happened, the tension in Web grew rather than lessened. Something had to break soon, but he had no idea in what direction to look for it.

Then it happened. Becky rode into his place shortly after breakfast. Her horse had been running hard, and her face was streaked with tears.

"What's wrong, Becky?" Web ran out to the spot where she had dragged her horse to a halt. "Something happen to Gil?"

"Yes," she said, and Web heard anger, not

sorrow or fear, in her voice. "Something happened to Gil. His weak knees folded up on him."

Web helped Becky from the saddle. "What do you mean?"

"Gil sold out to the land company."

A kick in the stomach wouldn't have jarred Web more.

"He said he wouldn't," Web said, seeking words to voice his anger and not say anything that would hurt Becky even more.

"He says a lot of things," Becky said. "Maybe he means them when he says them. But when real pressure is put on him, he takes the easiest way out, no matter who gets hurt."

"What are you going to do now, Becky?"

"Gil made arrangements for us to stay right on our place and look after it for Tree."

Web saw a ray of hope. "Maybe I'll still have a way out."

"Don't count on it," Becky said. "Gil will take the easy way again. And bucking orders from Sim Dalbow isn't the easy way. You know that."

Anger surged up in Web again. "Bucking me may not be too easy, either."

"Let's wait and see what happens, Web. Maybe things will work out. We've got to hope so."

Web nodded numbly. He knew things wouldn't work out. And so did Becky. Gil Harris had sold more than his farm when he had sold out to the land company. He had sold his soul.

VI

It was afternoon before Web found any reason to go to town. He expected to be challenged when he crossed Gil Harris' land. He could easily have postponed his trip into Bell, but he wanted to see what form the challenge was going to take.

He passed the house, but he saw no movement. He was sure Becky was inside, but she didn't show herself. He wondered where Gil was. Maybe he had been ordered to stop Web.

But it wasn't Gil who confronted Web a quarter of a mile below the house. Jess Rakaw was sitting on his horse in the middle of the road, waiting for Web, as he came around a bend in the road where it followed the banks of the creek.

"Reckon you know you're trespassing," Rakaw said as Web reined up.

"Hadn't figured it that way," Web said.

"Well, start figuring it that way. Tree land is off bounds for you. And you're on Tree land now."

"I understood that Gil sold out to the land company."

Rakaw nodded. "He did. But Tree is operating the land for the company right now. And we don't want trespassers."

"That could lead to some sticky situations," Web said, watching Rakaw tensely.

"Reckon it could," Rakaw said. "That's up to you."

"In that case, it may get real sticky. I need to go to town now and then, and when I do, I'm going through here. What do you figure to do about it?"

"Stop you."

"Beginning right now?"

Web kept his hand close to the butt of his gun. He didn't know how fast Jess Rakaw was. But he might find out any second now. One thing was sure: neither Rakaw nor any other Tree hand was going to turn him back. They might kill him, but that was the only way they'd stop him from going through.

Rakaw stood his ground, studying Web carefully. Then he eased the reins on his horse and nudged him out of the road.

"Time enough later," he said. "You'll have to go to town more than once. Next time maybe you won't make it."

For a moment Web considered forcing the issue. But he thought better of it and nudged his horse into a slow walk. As he came even with Rakaw, he looked at the sneer on the puncher's face.

"It won't be any easier next time, Rakaw," he said.

Rakaw swore, and Web thought he was going to draw. But he didn't, and Web rode on down the road and off Harris' land.

In town, Web rode up to the hitchrack in front of Farnsworth's store and dismounted. Inside the store, he went back to the spot where Valaree was working. There really wasn't anything important that he wanted in town. He'd just had to satisfy himself that Tree would actually try to stop him from using the road across Harris' land.

"How are the land company books coming?" Web asked.

Valaree looked up sharply. "What are you talking about, Web? I keep books for Mr. Farnsworth."

"And the land company," Web said. "Farnsworth's business couldn't keep you as busy as you seem to be."

Valaree shot a glance at Farnsworth in his usual rocking chair behind the counter. "All right. So I keep books for the land company, too. Let's let it go at that."

Web knew the subject was closed. If he pushed it farther, he'd be jeopardizing what was left of the bond between Valaree and him.

"You know they bought out Gil Harris," he said.

She nodded. "I know. What are you going to do, Web? The land company and Tree have you surrounded."

"Surrounded but not surrendered," Web said.

Impulsively she reached over and squeezed his hand. "I hope they don't make you surrender," she said softly.

"It will be a longer day than they've seen before I knuckle down," he said.

Farnsworth was scowling at them as though he thought Web was taking up too much of Valaree's time, for which he was paying. But Web was in no mood to let Farnsworth's likes or dislikes have any influence on him.

Another interruption came, however, that did destroy the mood Valaree had set. Ivan Sitzman charged into the store, looking around quickly until he saw Web. Then he came toward the back of the store on a trot.

"Somebody stole every cow critter I had," he said to Web.

Web frowned, as much at the interruption as at the news. "Any idea who did it?"

"Sure," Sitzman said. "And so do you if you give it a thought. Tree stole them."

"What would Tree want with your stock, Ivan?"

But even as he asked, he knew. And he knew Sitzman was right in blaming Tree. Sitzman's cattle were scrubs, the kind so many homesteaders had. Tree wouldn't want them mixed in with the good cattle on the ranch. But if Sitzman lost his cattle, he'd be hard put to get through the drought.

"Ask another silly question, and I won't even bother to answer," Sitzman snapped. "They stole the cattle for the same reason they burned Ekhart's barn."

"Let's take a look on Tree and see if we can

find your cattle."

Sitzman nodded. "That's why I was looking for you. I came by your place, but you weren't home. Then when I rode through Gil's place, Rakaw had the nerve to try to stop me and tell me I was trespassing. Another word from him and I'd have blown his head off."

Web looked at Sitzman. He wasn't even wearing a gun. "What with?" he asked.

"I carry a rifle on my saddle," Sitzman said. "Anyway, he let me by. I figure I'll have to have your help to get my cattle. But we'd better move fast, or those rustlers will push them off into the sand hills to the south and I'll never find them."

"All right," Web said. "Let's go."

"Be careful," Valaree said softly as Web turned to leave.

"I'll do that," Web promised.

At the hitchrack, Sitzman voiced a question. "Which way will we go? Looks like we'll hit trouble if we cut across Gil's place."

"We'll go the shortest route," Web said, in no mood to sidestep any conflict. "That will be across Gil's place, my place and Tree's home ranch. We might as well face up to trouble one time as another."

Sitzman nodded. "Suits me. It's coming to a showdown sooner or later, anyway."

There was no one to challenge them on the road up the creek through Gil Harris' land. They crossed Web's place, stopping only long enough for Web to get Sitzman some extra ammunition for his rifle.

They passed the Tree buildings and were soon on the land south of Billy McNeil's farm.

"Where do you figure they'll be?" Web asked.

"They were home this morning," Sitzman said. "I milked my two cows then. So they shouldn't be too far away. Probably just south of my place somewhere."

"Maybe they just wandered off," Web suggested.

"Sure they did," Sitzman said. "But they had help. My south fence is cut—every wire."

Web saw a rider top a rise off to the southwest and reined his horse that way.

Before they reached the knoll where the rider had appeared, Web and Sitzman rode down into a swale where about thirty head of cattle were grazing. Web reined up.

"See any of your stuff here?" he asked.

Sitzman nodded. "That brindle there is one of

my milk cows. And that red and white spotted cow is the other one. That brockle face is mine, too. Reckon all of mine are mixed in with those critters here."

"Let's cut them out," Web said. "And we'd better hurry."

Sitzman nodded. "I saw that rider, too. Let's go."

But they had only two of Sitzman's cows cut out of the little herd when three riders came over the rise to the south and galloped down on them.

"We've got company," Web said, checking Sitzman as he started after another of his cows.

Sitzman eased his rifle around across the saddle horn. "Guess we'd better visit a spell."

The riders came on down the slope and reined up sharply. Sim Dalbow was in the lead, with Ray Hickman and another scowling man only half a length behind him.

"Stealing cows now, are you?" Dalbow said through clenched teeth, his hand resting only inches from his gun.

"We're taking back what you already stole," Sitzman retorted.

Dalbow gripped the butt of his gun. "Are you calling me a thief?"

Sitzman didn't flinch. "That's up to you. Just explain how my cows got into this herd unless somebody drove them here."

"Show me your brand on them," Dalbow said. "If you can prove they're yours, you can have them."

Sitzman swore. "You know none of us little farmers brand our cows."

"That's so you can appropriate any unbranded calves or strays you find and claim them as your own," Dalbow said. "Well, it won't work this time. These critters are on Tree land, and unless you can show your own brand on them, they're going to stay here."

Web gently reined his horse back, pulling away from Sitzman.

"You're spoiling for a fight, Dalbow," Web said. "Why?"

"I'm not prodding anybody," Dalbow said. "But I'm not about to sit here with my hands folded while a couple of stinking sodbusters steal Tree beef."

"These aren't Tree critters, and you know it."

"Do I?" Dalbow said softly. "I don't see any other brand on them."

"You don't see the Tree brand on them, either."

Web shot a glance at Sitzman. He was still tense and ready, although Web had taken the play away from him. Then Web turned his attention back to the three Tree hands, still bunched together but spread out enough so that each had room to handle his gun.

Time had run out as far as it could go, Web knew. Dalbow and Hickman had come to fight, and they weren't going to be stalled much longer. The third man was a question. He would probably fight, but he didn't show the eagerness the others did.

Web heard it first, the pounding hoofs of a running horse. The concentration of the others wasn't broken for another minute; then Dalbow jerked his head up, cocked to one side like a bird's.

Web still didn't take his eyes off Dalbow and Hickman. Only when he saw their attention falter did he turn to see who had stopped the thunder of guns in the swale.

Eli Blaine was bearing down on them from the direction of Tree headquarters. Web guessed that he had seen Sitzman and Web ride past on their way there. He didn't look like the beaten man

Web had last seen as he left Tree the other morning. Anger was riding with him as he prodded his horse toward the five men.

"What's going on here?" he shouted as he jerked his horse to a sliding halt.

"We came after Sitzman's cows," Web said when Dalbow didn't answer.

"What are they doing here?"

"These sodbusters are trying to steal some unbranded critters," Dalbow said. "They can't prove they belong to Sitzman."

"They sure don't belong to Tree," Web said.

"Simmer down, you hotheads!" Eli shouted, then reined his horse toward the little herd of cattle. In a minute he was back.

"See any brands?" Dalbow asked sourly.

"No," Eli said. "And if you put a Tree brand on a skinny critter like that brockle face or that brindle, I'll shoot it myself. I don't know whether they belong to Sitzman or not, but I want those cattle off my land right now. They're a disgrace to Tree." He scowled at Dalbow. "What do you mean, trying to claim bone racks like that? Tree runs only good cattle."

"Isn't that just dandy?" Dalbow snapped.

Web scowled. The danger of a clash with the

Tree hands was past now. But he was seeing something he had never expected to see: disrespect in Sim Dalbow for Eli Blaine.

"Cut those scrub cattle out of my herd," Eli ordered.

Dalbow looked at the two men with him. Then he jerked a thumb at Web and Sitzman. "They came to do that job. Let them do it."

He wheeled his horse and galloped off to the south, Hickman and the other Tree rider following. Web turned to look at his father. Eli's face was as dark as a thundercloud.

"Get those scrawny critters off my land and don't let them set foot over here again!" he shouted. "I'll shoot them myself if I catch them on Tree land again."

Web wheeled toward the herd, helping Sitzman cut out the dozen cattle that belonged to **him.**

VII

Uneasiness rode with Web after he left Sitz-man's place, where they had put the cattle back in the pasture and mended the fence. It wasn't uneasiness at the way Dalbow had obviously asked for a fight today, although that threatened real trouble in the near future. It was Eli who worried Web.

Eli Blaine had been the iron-handed rule of Tree as long as the ranch had been in existence. Today that iron rule was gone. Dalbow had backed off from pushing the thing to a head, but he had defied Eli's orders, and Eli hadn't done a thing about it. Web had considered Tree with Eli at its head a formidable enemy. But with Eli no longer cracking the whip, Tree was much more dangerous. Today's threat of gun play was proof of that.

Web tossed on his bed for an hour after he blew out his lamp, trying to think of a way to stop the Bell County Land Company from swallowing up every farm along the creek.

The land company's plan was clear in Web's mind now. He was hemmed in himself. It was only a matter of time until he'd have to knuckle under, unless he could find some means of escape. There were other tough settlers along the creek—Sitzman, Billy McNeil, Ed Ekhart. But Web thought he saw the pattern for them, too.

It didn't make sense that they would be gunned down, not in this day of civilized law. But there could be no denying that today out there on Tree south of Ivan Sitzman's farm, that had been the intention. Sitzman was to have been eliminated right there. And if Eli hadn't come along when he did, the deed would surely have been carried out. Web would probably have gone down, too.

Then what would have happened? Would Billy McNeil and Ekhart had held out when they saw the result of opposing the powers that be? Web doubted it. Neither man was so stubborn that he was willing to die for his little plot of land. And that could be the alternative to getting out.

But if the land company couldn't get the mortgages on those homesteads, maybe that would slow things up a little. Not every farmer was selling to the company. Many were just pulling out, leaving their land to the bank, which held the mortgage. If the bank refused to sell those mortgages to the company, it might buy a little time for Web to try once more to organize the settlers.

Web half expected to be stopped the next morning when he rode across Gil Harris' land to town. If Tree wanted to force the issue, Web was ready. The time for sidestepping was past. But there was no challenge, and Web rode on down the creek to Bell unmolested.

The bank was just opening for business when Web reined up at the hitchrack. He went inside and crossed directly to the inner office of Fred Bell. Bell looked up as Web came in, and Web thought he saw lines in his face that hadn't been there a day or two before. Something was preying heavily on the banker's mind.

"What can I do for you, Web?" Bell asked, motioning to a chair.

"Plenty if you want to," Web said, seating himself. "You can stop selling these mortgages to the Bell County Land Company."

Bell frowned. "The bank has to have the money. I explained that to you the other day."

"Don't you have enough money to cover the withdrawal of Farnsworth in case he tries to wreck you that way?"

"Maybe," Bell said. "But it wouldn't leave me with any working capital."

"But you could keep your doors open," Web said with satisfaction. "Don't you see that if you keep turning these mortgages over to the company, that company will soon own everything in this county, including you and your bank?"

"Not my bank," Bell said. "I'm keeping it solvent."

"If Farnsworth and Eli get control of most of the farm land around here, what business can you do unless you bow and scrape to them?"

Bell got up and walked nervously to the litttle back window in his office. Web could see that it wasn't the first time he had thought of this. Evidently he realized that the land company had to be stopped, but he didn't have the nerve to do it.

"But what will happen if I refuse to sell any more mortgages to the company and Farnsworth decides to pull out his money? Then the little fellows will get panicky and demand their money, too. The bank will go under."

"That's a chance you'll just have to take," Web said. "It's a cinch that if the land company grabs control of most of this country, about the only customers you'll have will be Tree and Farnsworth. They'll tell you exactly what you can do and what you can't do. You might as well make up your mind. If you decide to make a stand now, at least you'll have a few of us to stand with you."

The banker chewed his lower lip. "All right," he said finally. "I'll take a chance. Farnsworth hasn't got me completely under his thumb yet, and I don't relish the idea of being put there. I won't sell any more mortgages to the land company. You'll stand by me?"

"With everything I've got," Web said.

But he was sure the banker knew that wouldn't be much. If Farnsworth pulled his money out of the bank and started the story the bank was shaky, nothing could save Fred Bell and his bank.

On the other hand, Farnsworth needed a bank. If he kept his money in his store, he'd leave himself wide open to robbery. With so many homesteaders drying out and their families hungry, money lying around to be had for the taking would be an almost irresistible temptation. Farnsworth might be afraid to pull his money out of the vault in the bank.

Web stopped at Ekhart's place on the way home to tell him what Bell had promised to do. But Ekhart was in his field, trying to cultivate crops that were practically nonexistent in the dry dust.

Halfway across Harris' place on his way home, Web was stopped by Gil Harris himself.

"I've been given orders to stop you from crossing this land," Harris said.

Web leaned over his saddle horn. "Look, Gil, I know you sold out to the land company. But that doesn't change the fact that you are my brother-in-law and we're friends. You won't stop me from riding across here."

"I've got to," Harris said, frowning. "I'm working for the company now. That was the only way I'd sell. They had to give me a job."

"They gave you a job you can't handle, Gil," Web said.

"You won't fight me," Harris said confidently.

"Think again," Web said. "I've got to come

across Tree land somewhere to get off my place. And you know I'm not selling out. So if anybody gets in my way, you know what will happen."

Harris shifted his weight from one foot to the other. "That's what Becky said you'd do."

"She knows me pretty well. How does she like the idea of you selling out?"

"It wasn't her idea," Harris admitted. "But she goes along with whatever I say."

Web ran a finger along his chin. "I think I'll ride over to the house and talk to her."

"She isn't there now," Harris said quickly.

"No? Where is she?"

"She's at Tree. I sent her there to be safe. I was afraid there might be trouble here, and I didn't want her to get hurt."

"Why do you figure there'll be trouble now, Gil?" Web asked. "You sold out to keep from getting into trouble, didn't you?"

Gil frowned and scratched his ear. "That was trouble I couldn't handle," he said finally.

"And you figure you can handle this? Don't bet on it, Gil."

Harris straightened his shoulders and took a deep breath. "You can't ride across my land any more, Web."

Web scowled, anger stirring in him. "Who is going to stop me?"

"I am," Harris said.

"Just be ready to do it, then, the next time I want to go to town, because I'm coming right down this road."

Web kicked his horse into a trot and rode on, not looking back. He knew he was leaving Gil Harris in an untenable situation. Harris apparently had been depending on Web refusing to fight with him when he agreed to carry out the land company's orders.

Web wasn't sure what Harris would do. He didn't have the backbone to fight if there was any way to avoid it. But the company had put him on the spot, and he probably would have to fight Web or the man the company would send to correct its mistake.

Web considered riding on to Tree to talk to Becky. It wasn't like Becky to run out on Gil, but Web knew that was what she had done. She must have reached the limit of her endurance of Gil's cowardice.

Web got his dinner, then decided on his next move. He wanted to bring Ed Ekhart up to date on what was happening, and he had to know just how far Gil Harris would go to carry out the orders the company had given him. Web wasn't at all sure what he would do if Gil did show fight. He couldn't gun down his sister's husband, even if she had left him. But neither could he allow Harris to stop him from riding across the land.

Getting his horse, he headed back toward Ekhart's place. He guided his horse along at an easy trot, every nerve alert. He didn't expect Harris to ambush him. Even that took more nerve than Harris had. Anyway, Gil Harris wasn't the kind of man who would shoot another man from ambush.

But Web couldn't be sure that the land company might not have another man there to help Harris back up his threat. Farnsworth and Tree had men who wouldn't bat an eye at shooting from ambush.

But no trap was sprung as Web moved along the road, coming even with Harris' house. He saw Harris out by the barn and knew that Harris saw him, but Gil made an obvious show of not looking his way, pretending he had no inkling that Web was there.

Web rode on, finding Ekhart at his house. He reined into the yard to tell him of developments.

Ekhart swore at the news that Harris had sold out to the company, but he swelled with confidence when Web told him that Fred Bell had agreed not to sell any more mortgages to the land company.

"If we can keep those land grabbers from getting any more farms, we'll lick them," Ekhart said. "If you need any help keeping the road open through Harris' place, just let me know. I'll come at him from this side."

"I won't have any trouble with Gil," Web said. "You might keep an eye out for Jube Altson riding this way from town, though."

"I'll do that," Ekhart said.

Web rode back home, this time not seeing Harris.

For three days Web worked around his place, wondering when things would break loose. The men behind the land company were not patient men. The company would make another move soon. Maybe Bell had relented and had agreed to sell more mortgages to the company. Web knew that a couple of settlers to the north were in the process of pulling stakes. Both were heavily in debt to the bank. The only way the land company could get their land would be to take the mortgages off the hands of the homesteaders.

Then they'd have to pay Bell the full price of the mortgages or make a deal with him. If Fred Bell stood by his promise to Web, there would be no deals. And Web was sure Farnsworth would never pay the full amount due the bank.

Even Billy McNeil failed to come by Web's place, and Web wondered if Tree had set up men to keep anybody from coming to his homestead. Impatience got the better of Web, and he saddled up and rode toward town. He'd talk to Fred Bell and find out what was going on.

Again he rode across Harris' land without a challenge. But he had barely reached town when Darlene Bell motioned to him from the front of the bank. Web reined in and dismounted.

"Something wrong, Darlene?" he asked quickly.

"I want to talk to you, Web," the girl said, glancing back at the bank.

"I was just going to put on the nose bag," Web said. "How about having dinner with me at the restaurant?"

She nodded quickly. "That sounds fine."

They walked toward the restaurant, Darlene's brown head coming just about to his shoulder. The street was almost deserted.

"Not many in town," he said.

"Never are any more. Not too many people left in the country, Web. The homesteaders are pulling out every day."

"Any more mortgages dropped in your dad's hands?"

Darlene nodded as they turned into the restaurant. "That's what I want to talk to you about."

Web led Darlene to a table, and when they were seated he looked across at her. Her brown eyes met his squarely and, even though his mind was on the possibility of trouble over the mortgages, he couldn't help admiring the perfection of her features and the smooth deep tan of her skin.

"Has your dad sold those mortgages to the land company?"

She shook her head. "He promised you he wouldn't. He doesn't go back on his promises."

"Then what's the trouble?"

"Ever since Dad told Farnsworth's man that he wouldn't sell any more mortgages, he's been getting threats."

Web frowned. "What kind of threats? Are they threatening to hurt him or rob the bank?"

"Neither one," Darlene said. "They're threatening to harm me. Dad is a braver man than anyone gives him credit for being. If they'd threatened to shoot him or rob his bank, he wouldn't flinch. He'd just put a guard on the bank and stand his ground. But he's an old softie about me."

"Can't blame him," Web said.

He saw her flush. "I've been telling him I can take care of myself," she said. "You know that nobody would dare harm me. The whole country would be up in arms."

"You're right about that," Web admitted. "But the stakes are higher than a lot of people realize. Control of this whole country hinges on how much land that company can legally control."

Darlene nodded. "I know. That means more to Dad than some people think, too. You know he's a proud man. If he knuckles under to Farnsworth now, he'll never have any more prestige here in Bell."

"That's right," Web agreed. "But I doubt if he'll risk any danger to you, even for the sake of his pride."

"He will," Darlene said positively. "I told him

he had to. It would make both him and me look like cowards if he backed down now. I'm not afraid of any of them."

"Sounds good, but I'm not sure it isn't foolish," Web said. "What do you figure your dad will do?"

"Just what he said he'd do. Hang onto those mortgages."

"You be careful, Darlene," he said. "Don't take any chances. I'll see if I can find the source of those threats and do something about them."

Something pulled Web's eyes to the window like a magnet, and he found himself staring straight into the angry eyes of Valaree Prescott. Apparently she had been passing the restaurant and had looked in, seen him with Darlene, and stopped to make sure she was seeing right.

He looked back at Darlene and surprised an odd speculative look on her face. But it was gone in an instant.

"You're the one who must be careful," she said. "Dad says this land company will stop at nothing to get what it wants. I'll take care of myself. But I'm afraid for Dad and you and for some of the other settlers."

VIII

After finishing his meal at the restaurant, Web considered going up to the store to talk to Valaree, but decided against it. She was in no mood now to accept any explanation. He also thought of facing Farnsworth and making him talk. But he knew he could do nothing with the fat storekeeper unless he used force. He might have better luck working on the other partner in the strange alliance, Eli Blaine.

It wasn't like Eli to use threats and blackmail to get what he wanted. Web doubted if Eli even knew about the threats to Darlene Bell. If Eli had had a hand in it, Web was sure he could make him put a stop to it. If he was innocent, probably Eli himself would do something about it once he learned of it.

Web rode home, alert again as he crossed Harris' land. But the ride stirred up nothing more startling than a prairie chicken that made his horse shy and sent Web's hand streaking to his gun in an involuntary reaction.

He didn't even stop at his soddy but kept on up the creek, riding through the orchard where he had had the fight with Rakaw and Hickman. There was no challenge as he rode into the big yard. Dismounting, he flipped the reins around the hitchrack and walked slowly toward the door.

After the events of the last few days he had no idea what kind of reception he might receive there. But nothing was going to stop him from talking to Eli if he could find him.

Finding him proved to be an easy matter. As he stepped up on the veranda, Eli jerked open the door and stood there, his shaggy gray head framed in the doorway.

"What's on your mind?" he demanded gruffly.

"I want to talk to you," Web said with equal gruffness.

Eli glared at him for a moment, then stepped back and let Web cross in front of him into the living room. Web found a chair without waiting to be invited and turned to watch Eli stride across to his favorite chair and drop into it.

"Talk," Eli said when he faced Web.

"Since when did you start using threats to get

what you wanted?" Web demanded.

Eli bristled. "I don't use threats."

"That's not the way I've been hearing it," Web said. "Darlene Bell tells me that Fred has been threatened harm if he doesn't sell the mortgages he holds on homesteads along the creek."

"Who's threatening him?"

"She didn't name names," Web said. "It seems they're threatening to harm Darlene. That's Fred Bell's soft spot, and everybody knows it."

Eli got up and glowered down at Web. "And you think I'm doing that?"

"It's somebody in the land company. You're part of that, aren't you?"

"Maybe," Eli said after a moment of hesitation. "But I don't threaten people, especially women."

"If you don't you'd better call off your hounds, because somebody in the land company is doing it."

Eli sank down in his chair again, suddenly an uncertain, groping old man.

"I'm not the only one in the company," Eli said.

"But you are boss, aren't you? At least you

pretend to be."

"Sure I'm boss," Eli said uneasily. "But there are a lot of men involved."

Web nodded grimly. Obviously Eli Blaine had lost all control of the men who were supposed to be taking his orders.

"Henry Farnsworth is in the land company with you, isn't he? Is he furnishing the money and you the gunmen?"

Eli stared at the huge fireplace for a minute, then turned troubled eyes on Web. "You're mighty close to being right," he said. "But Farnsworth is only loaning me the money. I'll pay him back every cent with interest once this drought is over. Then I'll be the kingpin of this whole valley just like I started out to be. Eli Blaine will be a name that will command respect all over the state."

Web looked at his father, standing straight again in front of the huge fireplace like a king in his regal robes. He had dreamed a dream of being the ruler of all he surveyed for so long that he had no trouble imagining it to be a reality.

Web frowned. He didn't want to pity his father. Pity was the last thing Eli Blaine would want, and it was the last thing Web had ever expected to feel for him. But it was there now inside Web, gnawing at him like a canker. He actually felt sorry for Eli and his big dreams. Only Eli seemed utterly blind to the fact that those dreams were already in shambles. In that moment Eli was king of everything around him.

Perhaps Henry Farnsworth was the real power in the valley now. Farnsworth had the money, and usually the man with the money wielded the power.

Or maybe it was Sim Dalbow. Dalbow, as foreman of Tree, had brought in the gunmen who were controlling the things that Farnsworth's money bought. Guns held a lot of authority in a raw country.

It might be Farnsworth; it might be Dalbow. But one thing Web was sure of—it wasn't Eli Blaine. The man who had once been king of the valley was still king, but in name only. Web wondered why he was still allowed to sit on his throne.

"Where's Dalbow?" he asked after Eli had gone back to his chair.

"I don't know," Eli admitted. "Out on the range somewhere, I reckon."

"Are you afraid of him?"

Eli came out of his chair again as if he'd been stung by a wasp. "Afraid of Sim Dalbow? He's the best friend I have! He's been with me seventeen years, been my foreman for fifteen, and he's never kicked over the traces like members of my own family have."

"In seventeen years you ought to get to know a man," Web said. "Dalbow strikes me as different from the way he used to be."

"He's not the one who is different," Eli said. "He's loyal to Tree."

"Where did he come from?" Web asked.

Eli frowned. "What are you getting at, Web? You know where he came from. He was with a trail drive up from Texas. Stopped here, looking for a permanent job. We hit it off first rate, so he stayed. A couple of years later I made him foreman of Tree. He's still that."

"After fifteen years as foreman of Tree, is he still satisfied?"

"I reckon he is. He's never said he wasn't."

"He's never said why he was with that trail drive coming up from Texas, either, has he?"

Eli stamped a foot. "He was earning a living just like you or I would have done if we'd been in his boots."

Web nodded. "Maybe. But where was Dalbow before he hooked onto that drive?"

"Now just a minute!" Eli snapped, moving over to glare down at Web. "Are you trying to say that Sim Dalbow was on the run when he came up from Texas? I don't think he was. If he had been, the law could have found him here. But I don't care what he was before he came here. He's been a good foreman and still is. Now what else do you want to talk about?"

"Nothing," Web said, getting out of his chair, "except that you might look into these threats they're making against the Bell family. Since you're listed as the big cheese in the land company, you're going to get the blame for anything that happens to the Bells."

Eli frowned. "Nothing will happen to them," he said, but Web heard no conviction in Eli's voice.

Web went back outside, feeling that he had accomplished nothing by his visit. He was convinced now beyond a doubt that Eli no longer held the reins on Tree. And if he no longer controlled the men on his own ranch, there was little chance that he carried any weight with the Bell County Land Company.

At the hitchrack, Web hesitated, one hand on the reins of his horse. There was no movement anywhere in the yard. Evidently all the men who rode for Tree were gone from the buildings. An idea was stirring in Web's mind and it offered such possibilities that he couldn't push it out.

He glanced back at the house. Eli was not in sight. Apparently Web had been dismissed completely. That was all to the good.

Leaving his horse tied at the hitchrack, Web crossed the yard to the bunkhouse. He remembered how particular Sim Dalbow was about his personal belongings. That was the right of any man. But Dalbow had shown unusual possessiveness. His rages were monumental if he found any man, new hand or old, sitting on his bunk or showing an interest in his personal things.

Web had thought about it occasionally when he was growing up on Tree. But curiosity had never crowded Web into investigating. After one encounter with Dalbow's fury, no other cowhand on Tree had shown any outward curiosity, either.

But now Web was more than just idly curious. Maybe Dalbow had some things in his possession that would throw some light on his past and also give a reason for his behavior now. It seemed worth the risk he was running to find out.

Inside the dim interior of the bunkhouse, Web stopped. There were two little rooms opening off the main room where the hands slept. One of these little rooms was reserved for mending bridles and small bits of gear. The other room belonged to the foreman. His bunk was situated in such a way that a man sitting or lying on it could see most of the activity going on in the main room.

Web went into Dalbow's room. He didn't particularly like poking around in another man's personal belongings. But the chance of finding a link to Dalbow's past made it seem worth the annoyance of burying his compunctions.

Under Dalbow's bed, Web found a sack stuffed with clothes. A quick look through them revealed nothing. Behind the sack of clothes a battered pair of saddle bags was jammed against the wall. Web pulled them out and flipped open the strap on one of the bags.

As soon as he reached inside, he know he had found what he was looking for. Several newspapers were folded inside the bag, and he lifted them out. The ones on top of the pile were fairly recent; those on the bottom were yellow with age.

Web began at the top, glancing rapidly over the headlines. The top one had an item circled with a pencil mark. It told of a Pete Frazee who had escaped from a prison in Colorado. He was wanted for horse stealing. Web guessed that Pete Frazee, under some other name, was probably working on Tree now or would appear as soon as Dalbow could find him.

The next item was more to the point. It was a wanted poster, describing John Randall, wanted for murder in Texas. The description drew a perfect picture of Jess Rakaw.

There were a couple of others at which Web glanced. One, although again the name wasn't the same, fitted the description of Ray Hickman. Web guessed that Dalbow had gone out and brought in these men, offering them sanctuary from the law in exchange for the use of their guns. It gave Dalbow a power over the gunmen that Eli and maybe even Farnsworth had no idea he possessed.

Web dug deeper. Finding out that Tree was harboring murderers and thieves confirmed Web's suspicions, but it wasn't the thing he was really looking for. Somewhere in those papers there might be something that would throw some light on Dalbow himself. The other clippings gave Web a better picture of Dalbow than he'd had. No man who was not planning something far outside the law would go out of his way as Dalbow had done to get men of such caliber around him.

Then, in three of the bottom papers, growing yellow with the years, he saw the headlines that told him his search was ended. The papers had been printed in Texas and were dated eighteen years before.

Carefully, Web spread out the first paper on the bunk and leaned over it to read the faded print. The headlines told of a bank hold-up in which the bank president, a prominent man in town, had been killed. Scanning the page, Web got the story of the hold-up. The man wanted for the robbery and murder was a man named Sam Demson. Web didn't need a second to translate that into Sim Dalbow.

Dalbow had been on Tree for seventeen years. For a year he could have dodged the law in Texas and Oklahoma Territory, then latched onto a drive up the trail to Nebraska, with no intention of ever going back. Getting in with Tree shortly after Eli had laid out the ranch, he had stayed, behaving himself and working hard for Eli, because he couldn't afford to do anything that would attract attention to himself.

But that bank hold-up and murder had been eighteen years ago. Surely by now Dalbow must feel fairly safe from Texas law. Maybe now he thought he could safely begin reaching out for more illegal gains. Certainly Eli had laid the opportunity right in his lap with his greedy land grab.

Web put the papers back in the saddle bags, thinking that Sim Dalbow was a real egomaniac. Only a man who was very proud of his accomplishments would keep clippings like this when he dared not let anyone see them. Web tried to decide what a man like Sim Dalbow would do in the present situation. Would he go along with Eli's scheme and help Eli grab the country for Tree? Or would he help Farnsworth, who had the money to make it worth his while? Or would he work some scheme to get it all for Sim Dalbow? Web couldn't get that last possibility out of his mind.

Then suddenly he was jerked out of his speculations by the sound of hoofbeats in the yard. Some of the men must be coming back from work. Web slammed the saddle bags back under Dalbow's bunk and stepped out into the main room of the bunkhouse, every nerve keyed for action. No matter which of the tree hands had come back to the ranch, he wasn't going to like the idea of Web's snooping around the men's bunks while they were gone.

Web had almost reached the door when he heard boots crunching on the hard ground outside. He stepped into the doorway to be met by the blazing eyes of Jess Rakaw. Web shot a glance past him. But there was just one horse at the hitchrack beside his own.

"What are you doing in there?" Rakaw demanded.

"Just looking around," Web said.

He knew that he was not going to be able to quiet the suspicions in Rakaw's pale blue eyes.

"You've been snooping," Rakaw accused; "poking your nose into things that are none of your business."

"Maybe it is my business," Web said.

Rakaw was silent for a minute, his shoulders hunched forward, his eyes boring into Web. Web

watched the expression on his face as the gunman became convinced that Web had learned
things about him that he couldn't let leave the
ranch.

"You found some papers, didn't you?" Rakaw
asked.

Web didn't answer; he didn't have to. Rakaw
was convinced. Web knew that he'd never ride
away from Tree alive unless he left Rakaw dead
behind him.

"I asked you a question," Rakaw said. "What
did you find out?"

"Enough," Web said. "What are you going to
do about it?"

Web didn't exaggerate his chances. Rakaw
was a gunman; Web hadn't tried for speed with
his gun for a long time. But there was only one
way out of that yard for either of them now. That
was past the dead body of the other.

Rakaw's move was fast. Web knew his draw
couldn't match it. But the hate and eagerness to
kill that drove the gunman made him over-anx-
ious, and his first bullet dug some leather out of
the top of Web's boot as it snapped past, too far
to the right and too low.

Web, steeling himself to take more time, didn't

waste his first bullet. It was ahead of Rakaw's second shot. That shot, fired as Rakaw staggered off balance, snapped harmlessly past Web's head. Web's second bullet found its mark, too. For Rakaw, there was no third shot.

The door of the big house burst open as the din in the yard died away. Web slowly holstered his gun as he saw both Eli and Loretta Blaine rush out onto the veranda.

Then suddenly the yard was full of horses as the rest of the Tree crew galloped in and pulled up in a cloud of dust. Out of the dust came Sim Dalbow, his gun in his hand.

"What happened here?" he roared.

Eli yelled at him before Web could say a word, "Rakaw and Web had a fight."

"What about?" Dalbow demanded.

"I don't know," Eli said, coming down into the yard, his voice dropping to its normal pitch. "But you know how hot-headed Rakaw was. No telling what he blew up about."

Dalbow stared from Rakaw's body to Web. "Jess was fast with his iron," he said slowly. "You're not that fast."

"He was faster," Web said. "But he didn't shoot straight."

"Jess had a reason, you can bet on that," Dalbow said, his voice rising as he turned to look over the men behind him. "This is a case for the law to look into."

Web knew what Dalbow had in mind. Web would never get to the sheriff if Dalbow started to take him in. Web wasn't the only one to think that, apparently. Eli stepped up to face his foreman.

"You were close enough to see the whole thing, Sim. You know it was a fair fight." Eli faced the rest of the men. "Anybody here disagree?"

For a long minute the men stared from Eli to Dalbow; then, seeing that Dalbow evidently wasn't going to buck Eli, they slowly began shaking their heads.

"All right," Eli said. "I'll ride in and tell the sheriff myself. And I expect every man here to swear it was an even draw." He wheeled on Web. "You'd better get out of here."

Web nodded and strode to his horse, swinging into the saddle. As he rode out of the yard, he looked at Dalbow. The foreman's slate gray eyes were following every move he made, naked hate and suspicion mirrored in them.

IX

Sleep was an elusive thing for Web that night. How much did Eli know about what was going on at Tree? Just how much did Web himself actually know, and how much was he guessing? He had no proof that Dalbow was bringing in gunmen without Eli's knowledge and, even if that was true, it didn't prove that Dalbow was plotting against Eli.

Morning came with Web bone weary from lack of sleep. But there were things to do, and they pressed on Web's mind, driving out the weariness. He had to talk to Farnsworth. The fat storekeeper wouldn't tell him anything worth-while in so many words. But Web was willing to gamble that he could learn things by watching the pudgy face of the storekeeper.

Web wanted to know if Farnsworth knew

about the kind of men Dalbow was bringing in. If so, the true alignment was probably Dalbow and Farnsworth against Eli. If not, it was probably Dalbow and his gunmen against the whole Dutchmen Valley. And Web wouldn't want to lay any odds against Dalbow's gunmen.

The town was quiet when Web rode in. He glanced at the bank as he rode past on his way to Farnsworth's store, but he didn't stop. He hoped that Fred Bell was standing by his promise not to sell any more mortgages.

He reined up at the store, thinking of Valaree. He hadn't seen her since yesterday when he had surprised her looking through the restaurant window at Darlene Bell and him.

Inside the store, he crossed to the counter and looked over at the empty rocking chair. He seldom saw that chair without Farnsworth rocking idly in it. He went on to the back of the store, where Valaree was hard at work on her books.

"Where's Farnsworth?" he asked bluntly.

Valaree looked up as impersonally as if he were a total stranger. "He left the store a few minutes ago. I don't know where he went."

"Or when he'll be back?"

She shook her head. "He doesn't tell me every

move he makes."

"I thought maybe he did," Web said, and was surprised at the flush that swept over her face. She turned an angry look on him.

"I just work here. I don't own the store or Mr. Farnsworth."

"I can't imagine anyone wanting to own him," Web said. He sat down on a packing case a few feet from Valaree's desk. "Has he been buying any more mortgages from Bell?"

"That is none of my business or yours," she said sharply. "Ask Darlene."

He studied Valaree's flushed face as she bent over her books. "I might do that. Yesterday she was telling me Fred Bell was receiving threats because he had refused to sell any more mortgages."

"Was that all she was telling you?" Valaree asked caustically without looking up.

"Would that make any difference to you?"

"None whatsoever!"

"She said they were threatening to harm her, not Fred," Web said.

Valaree looked up then, her angry eyes defiant. "I suppose you think Mr. Farnsworth is making those threats. Maybe that's where he is now."

Web shook his head. "I doubt if Farnsworth himself is making any threats. But I'll wager he knows who is. Am I right?"

Valaree bent back over her books, but Web was sure she wasn't seeing a single figure on the page. "Ask Mr. Farnsworth."

"I would if he was here," Web said. "A lot of innocent people are getting pushed off their land, and a lot more are going to get squeezed off if something isn't done to stop it. I don't think you want that to happen, Valaree."

She flashed a straight look at him. "You don't know what I want. Besides, there isn't anything I can do."

"You can tell me what you know about this Bell County Land Company."

"I just keep books, that's all," Valaree said, frowning at her books again. "It's my job. A bookkeeper doesn't tell what she finds in the books. That just isn't done."

"If there is something crooked going on, what's so wrong about exposing it?"

"Who said there was anything crooked going on?" Valaree said sharply, her defiance rushing back.

Web slid off the packing box. "You don't know when Farnsworth will be back?"

"Haven't the slightest idea."

"Don't bother to tell him I was here," Web said as he started toward the door. "I'll be back sometime when he is here."

Web rode out of town, convinced that he was on the right track. Valaree knew a lot of things that he was only guessing. If she would only tell him what she knew, it might be that he could spread the jaws of the trap closing in on him and the other homesteaders along the creek. If he didn't do something soon, those jaws would clamp shut and the land company, whether that be Eli Blaine and Tree or Farnsworth and Dalbow, would rule supreme over the entire Dutchman Valley.

Again he crossed Gil Harris' land without a challenge. But he got little satisfaction from that. It was a cat and mouse game, and he was the mouse. Probably the land company figured it wasn't worth risking the life of a man to stop Web from crossing the land now. But any time it became necessary, they could put a block on the road and stop Web with guns if need be.

Web wasn't surprised to see Billy McNeil come

by late that afternoon. Billy hadn't been around lately, so he was due for a visit. But there was an unusual excitement in his face as he reined up in the yard.

"Saddle your horse, Web," he said. "You've got a date tonight."

Web set down the bucket he had been carrying. "Who is the date with? You?"

Billy grinned. "I reckon we can both figure out something more exciting than that. You've got a date with Valaree."

"Funny I hadn't heard about it." Web looked sharply at his friend. "Why are you beating around the bush? You've got something up your sleeve. Let's have it."

"I don't know as much about it as you do, I reckon," Billy said. "I was in town. Valaree saw me go by Farnsworth's store and came out to see me. Said she wanted to talk to you alone."

"That's nice," Web said, trying to hide his excitement. "I suppose she wants me to ride back to town tonight."

"No. She wants to meet you outside of town."

Excitement began to build higher in Web. Maybe Valaree had decided to tell him what she had learned from those books. If so, it was reasonable that she would want to get as far away from Henry Farnsworth and his gunhand, Jube Altson, as possible.

"Where am I to meet her?"

"At my place," Billy said.

Web frowned. "Your place? If she was going to pick some homestead, why not Niccum's or Ekhart's? They're close to town. Your place is a long way out."

"I reckon I'm to blame for that," Billy said apologetically. "She said she had to get out of town where nobody would know she was meeting you. All I could think of was my place. She wouldn't dare come here to your place. I suggested she come to my farm tonight and I'd have you there. She agreed."

Web nodded. It was reasonable that Billy should suggest his own place, and Valaree was probably ready to accept any solution that appeared safe. Certainly Billy's farm would be about the last place in the valley anyone would expect her to go when she left town.

"I'll get my horse," Web said. "When will she be there?"

"She said she'd slip out of town as soon after work as she could get away without being seen."

"This may be the night we get the information about the land company we've been digging for," Web said, excitement rushing through his blood.

The sun wasn't down yet when Web and Billy rode up to Billy's little sod house. Since Billy had no wife to demand a better house, he was content with just two small rooms. The barn was a better building, Web thought, than the house.

"If I ever get married," Billy had said, "my wife will want a new house, anyway. This is good enough for me now.

Behind the barn was a little pasture where Billy turned his saddle horse when he wanted to keep him close. Web and Billy turned their horses into the pasture, then went inside. Billy fried some potatoes and a couple of thick slabs of ham.

When they had eaten and washed the dishes, Web went to the door and peered out at the road leading from town.

"She'll be here," Billy said, laughing. "You're as nervous as a cat in a coyote den. She probably can't get away till dark, and it's quite a ride out here."

Web turned back. "Reckon you're right. But this can mean a lot to us if things go as I hope."

He dropped down on one of the boxes that served as chairs when the one good chair was in use. Somehow Web couldn't quiet his nerves. So many things could go wrong.

"Stop stewing," Billy advised. "She'll be here. Even if she doesn't come, we're no worse off than before."

An hour dragged by, then another. Web's uneasiness increased. If Valaree was coming, surely she would have been there by now. He knew how she hated tardiness. Something must have happened. Web was just ready to suggest they go look for her when he caught the sound of hoofbeats.

"She's coming," Billy said excitedly, leaping to his feet.

Web started toward the door, then stopped, listening. "That's not just one horse. That's a whole herd."

"You're right," Billy agreed, alarm in his voice.

Billy grabbed his rifle from its hooks close to the door, and Web stepped to the door, his gun in his hand. It was too dark outside to see how many riders were coming or who they were. But Web had no trouble locating the sound. The rid-

ers were coming down the slope to the left of the
road, keeping the barn between them and the
house.

"Trouble," Billy said softly. "I can smell it."

Web nodded. "Could be Tree. Or maybe Jube
Altson leading a pack of gunmen."

"Suppose they know you're here?"

Web had been thinking the same thing. But
there was no time now to speculate on that. Three
quick shots ripped through the night, and the
bullets thudded into the sod walls of the house.

"They mean business," Web said. "Douse the
light!"

Before Billy could blow out the light, a bullet
smashed into the pans hanging by the stove, coming through the open square in the wall that
served as a window. Billy had a door that fitted
into the opening when he wanted to close it
against the weather, but it wasn't in place now.

"Those shots aren't meant just to scare us,"
Billy said, coming back to Web after blowing out
the lamp.

Web nodded. "They intend to put you out of
business."

It was evident from the start that it was going
to be a one-sided battle. The raiders remained far

out in the night, sniping away at the house, keeping the two men inside pinned down. Web and Billy answered the shots, but they realized they were wasting their powder.

Suddenly a pillar of flame leaped up from the barn, lighting the whole yard. The raiders had touched off the dry hay inside the barn, and it was blazing furiously.

"Burning my barn like they did Ekhart's," Billy said, and fired two more shots at the elusive targets. "I'd like to blow their heads off!"

Web watched the men out beyond the yard. Why didn't they leave now that they had fired the barn? They had hit Ekhart and ridden away before he could do anything about it. But the riders were still out there. Web could see them, although they didn't offer much of a target.

Then a sound at the back of the house made him wheel and dash for the hole in the wall that served as a window for the bedroom. But he wasn't fast enough. A flaming torch made of rags soaked in coal oil tied around a stick came hurtling through the open window. It landed on the bed, and the flame leaped up hungrily toward the roof.

"They're burning us out like rats!" Billy

shouted.

Web took quick stock of the situation. The house was sod; the walls wouldn't burn. But the things inside would burn. And the roof was boards covered with a layer of tar paper held down by a thick layer of sod. Burning from underneath like this, that wood and tar paper would blaze away merrily, making the inside of the house an inferno.

Before he left the bedroom, Web saw the rider spurring away and fired a shot through the window. He knew a moment of satisfaction as he saw the rider sit bolt upright, then grab the saddle horn as he rode on out of sight. At least that one raider would carry away a memento of the raid.

But that did nothing to solve the immediate problem. Web and Billy couldn't stay in the house much longer. There was only one bucket half full of water there. That would do no more than make the fire sputter a little.

Web looked out toward the front of the house again. The riders were still out there; in fact, they were moving closer. At Ekhart's, the raiders had hit and run. They weren't running this time; they were waiting. And they could have only one reason for that.

"They're aiming to kill us when we come out," Billy said tightly, voicing Web's thoughts.

"Looks that way."

Something cold and hard was gnawing at Web's insides as he tried to think of some way to escape this trap. A rider came close to the barn, and Web guessed it was to keep the blaze of the burning hay from shutting off his view of the house. Billy fired at the rider, hitting the horse. The horse pitched forward, then struggled to his feet again, leaving his rider afoot. The man ran wildly back toward the other riders, Billy hurrying him along with more shots from his rifle.

Then another gun spoke from the knoll to the west. Web heard it, noting its heavier boom. Immediately he saw the consternation it created among the riders beyond the barn. One man there was swaying in his saddle, testifying to the fact that the unknown rifleman wasn't firing warning shots.

The raiders turned their attention to the new menace, and Web raced for the door, motioning for Billy to follow. If ever they were to have a chance to escape the fire trap, this had to be it. Web had heard only one rifle out there on the knoll. If there was just one man, it would take the raiders only a short time to dispose of him or assign two men to drive him back while the rest tended to their original business.

Web and Billy dashed through the door and zigzagged across the yard to the shadows beyond the light from the fire. No shots interrupted their flight as the raiders, surprised by the attack on their flank, concentrated on the new menace.

Billy had dumped a small pile of posts in the yard to be used in his corral fence. Web and Billy reached this pile and flopped down flat behind it. Web's Colt was almost worthless at that range, but he emptied the gun anyway, holding the sights high. Billy's rifle was more effective.

Caught in the crossfire from the rifleman on the knoll and Billy's rifle from the pile of posts, the raiders quickly reconsidered their plans and wheeled their horses, disappearing across the creek to the south.

Web and Billy strayed behind the posts until they were sure the raiders were gone. Then they stood up cautiously, guns still ready in case some determined man had stayed behind. They heard a rider coming slowly down from the knoll to the west and turned to face him. Web wasn't surprised when he recognized Ivan Sitzman riding into the yard.

"This is a pretty mess," Sitzman grunted, looking at the burning house and barn. "They're out to kill us now if we don't leave, I reckon."

"Glad you happened along," Web said. "We were in a tight spot."

"I didn't just happen along," Sitzman said. "I was in bed when I heard the first shot. It's only a quarter of a mile over to my place, you know. When I saw the fire, I grabbed my pants and rifle and got over here as fast as I could. I winged one of the gents pretty good."

Web surveyed the fires. "We can't save anything in either building. You'd better come home with me, Billy."

Billy nodded. "I reckon. But if they think they can have my place now, they can think again. I'll hole up over here and pick off every one that sets foot on my land."

"What about your stock?" Sitzman asked. "Want to run it over to my place? I'll keep an eye on it for you."

"Sounds good," Billy said. "But how long will it be before they burn you out?"

Sitzman shook his head grimly. "Don't know. I reckon I'll be right there waiting for them when they come. I'll kill me a few fire bugs or know the reason why."

It was decided to leave Billy's cattle where they were for the night. Sitzman would come over in the morning and get them, and Billy would come back to help. Right now, they'd take the horses out of the little pasture, and Billy would ride home with Web for the night.

Web's thoughts were already reaching ahead. The raid on Billy's place hadn't been made just to wipe out Billy's homestead, although it had practically accomplished that. Web was convinced the raiders had known that he was there with Billy, and the raid had been for the double purpose of destroying Billy's homestead and Web.

Web and Billy were the two ringleaders in the fight to organize the homesteaders against the big squeeze of the land company. If tonight's raid had been successful, there would have been little to stand in the way of the land company's complete grab of Dutchman Valley. Sitzman and Ekhart might stand pat, but they could easily be disposed of, once Web and Billy were out of the way.

The question that pestered Web was how the

raiders had known that he was at Billy's place. Only one person had knowledge of the proposed meeting, as far as Web knew. Valaree.

Maybe he was wrong about her. Maybe she was hand in glove with Farnsworth, and the incident tonight had been part of a master plan. Perhaps Valaree was a big wheel in the land company, too. Web shook his head. He couldn't believe that. But it was too much of a coincidence to overlook that Valaree hadn't shown up and the raiders had come instead. There was no escaping the fact that it had been a well laid trap. Somebody had some explaining to do, and Web was going to start finding out who in the morning at Farnsworth's store.

As soon as breakfast was over the next morning, Billy rode back to his place to help Ivan Sitzman take care of the cattle. Web saddled up and headed for town.

The town was quiet as usual when he rode in and reined up at the hitchrack in front of Farnsworth's store. He doubted if Farnsworth himself would be at the store yet. He wasn't an early riser. Valaree said she usually opened the store in the mornings and took care of the few early customers. If Valaree was in the store alone now, that would suit Web fine. What he had to say was for her ears only.

As soon as he stepped inside, he knew that luck was with him. Valaree was behind the counter instead of working with her books at the back of the store. The big rocker was empty. There were no customers in the store, either.

Web crossed to the counter, watching Valaree's face for a sign of surprise that he was still among the living. He saw doubt and hesitation there but no real surprise.

"You were a little late for your appointment last night, weren't you?" Web asked, his anger making the question blunt and impersonal.

Valaree colored a little. "I couldn't get out of town. Somebody took my horse out of the livery barn. Ned wouldn't tell me who. And he wouldn't rent me a rig of any kind. I tried, Web."

"So did somebody else. They had better luck. Billy's place is burned to the ground. If it hadn't been for Ivan Sitzman, we'd have burned with it. Was that the way you planned it?"

Anger rushed into her face. Web tried to decide whether Valaree was angry at being accused of having had a hand in the raid or whether she was angry at being found out. The only thing he could be sure of was that her anger was real.

"If that's what you think," Valaree said, her hands gripping the edge of the counter till her knuckles showed white, "get out of here and don't ever come back!"

Web realized he had let his anger drive him too far. If he had used a softer approach, Valaree might have told him what she had planned to tell him last night—if she had been on the level then. Now she would tell him nothing, even if she had been sincere yesterday.

Web wheeled and strode out of the store, more uncertain than ever about Valaree's part in the raid last night. But whether she was guilty or not, he had tossed the fat in the fire. She wouldn't help him now.

X

Valaree watched Web walk out of the store, her fingers still gripping the edge of the counter till they hurt. She had never been so furious, she was sure. He had practically accused her of setting a trap for him and Billy McNeil last night.

As the minutes dragged by, her anger subsided It had been just as she had told Web. She had gone after her horse at the livery barn shortly before dark. Ned, the stable owner, had said her horse was gone, but he wouldn't say who had taken him or why. Neither would he rent her a rig or another horse.

Valaree was sure that he had just been obeying orders. Ned wasn't the kind of man who would deliberately deny her the use of a horse or rig unless he had definite instructions to do so. Valaree was also sure who had given Ned those orders.

But it wasn't until Web had come in that morning and said that Billy McNeil's place had been burned to the ground that she realized how serious the whole thing was.

Somehow someone, probably Jube Altson, had learned of her plan to ride out to Billy's place to talk to Web Blaine. The trap had been set then. Keeping her a prisoner in town was an important part of that trap.

Valaree walked to the door and watched Web mount his horse and spur him angrily down the street. She really couldn't blame Web for being angry. She would probably have felt the same in his place. But that didn't ease her own resentment. She had told him the truth, and he hadn't believed her. She bit her underlip. In other things she hadn't been honest with him, and he hadn't even suspected her duplicity.

She went back behind the counter and sat down on a stool there. Why had she relented yesterday and decided to tell Web what was going on? If she'd just been content to let things go on as they were, everything would have been all right. Now she had jeopardized her whole future. Any potential future she might have had with Web was gone. And as for her position with

Henry Farnsworth, that would be gone, too, if Farnsworth found out why she had wanted to see Web last night.

Henry Farnsworth came slowly up the street and into the store, puffing from the exertion of moving his huge bulk along the walk. Valaree tried not to think of an irritated duck every time she saw him walk, but the resemblance was too pronounced to ignore.

Farnsworth waddled over to his rocking chair behind the counter, took off his hat, hung it on a peg and sat down, mopping his bald head with his handkerchief.

Valaree moved down to her corner with her books, feeling Farnsworth's green eyes following her every move. Somehow she resented it. His eyes usually followed her as she moved around the store, and she didn't mind. In fact, she had actually cultivated the storekeeper's interest. A man with money such as Farnsworth had was not one to antagonize.

But this morning she couldn't help wondering what was going on behind those green eyes. Was Farnsworth thinking about Valaree's attempt to meet Web Blaine last night? If he suspected what she had planned to tell him, not only her relationship with Farnsworth but her very life might be in danger.

Valaree went to work with her books, although she had them up to date now. While pretending to be completely absorbed in her work, she noted everything that went on in the store. She noted particularly when Jube Altson came in.

Although she kept her pencil poised as though about to write down some figure, her entire attention followed Altson as he crossed to Farnsworth and began talking in a low voice. Farnsworth answered and kept his voice low, too, obviously to keep Valaree from hearing. But the intensity of feeling in their tones gave them a range they didn't suspect.

"You should have gotten them both even if you had to ride them down with your horses," Farnsworth snapped.

"We'd have done it but for Sitzman. We didn't know till later how many men were up there with rifles. We had to stop that shooting. He hit Jake pretty bad."

"So you turned tail and ran," Farnsworth said acidly. "I saw Blaine riding out of town this morning when I came to the store. He didn't look like he was even scratched."

"He'd have been dead if we'd had the chance to finish the job," Altson said. "We had the barn and house both burning. Blaine and McNeil had to come out in a minute or two, and we were waiting. Then Sitzman opened up."

Farnsworth nodded impatiently. "I've heard that before. We've got to get rid of those two. Sitzman, too. He's stuck his nose in too many times. With them out of the way, the rest will be easy."

Jube Altson straightened his big six-foot two-inch frame. "I'll take care of Blaine personally. Dalbow says Blaine has found out some things that could give us more trouble." He grinned. "Dalbow even offered me an extra fifty to beef Blaine."

Farnsworth waved a hand. "Don't worry about his fifty. You get rid of those three men any way you can; then come to me. I'll see that you get paid properly."

Farnsworth swung his gaze toward his book-keeper, and Valaree bent lower over her books. Farnsworth and his gunman talked some more, but their voices were even lower now, and Valaree couldn't hear what was being said.

When Altson left the store, Farnsworth sat for

a long time staring at Valaree. Although she didn't look up from her books, she was aware of his studied gaze. She wished he would say what he was thinking. If he knew what she had planned to tell Web Blaine, let him say so and be done with it. This uncertainty was almost as bad as being convicted.

Finally Farnsworth turned his attention to a little book he took from his pocket. Valaree kept her eyes on her work, but her mind was far from the figures she saw. What would Farnsworth do if he guessed that she had intended to betray his trust? She didn't want to think of the worst that could happen. At the very least, she would be fired. What would she do then? She'd had one avenue of escape all figured out if such a calamity should befall her. But that was gone now. Web Blaine would have nothing more to do with her. That was what came from playing both ends against the middle. Maybe she wasn't as clever a gambler as she had thought.

She had come to Bell to teach school. But her real ambition, admitted only to herself, had been to find adventure and to marry a rich man. She'd come there with the mistaken idea that there would be plenty of rich men and few women. She had known that the percentage of rich men compared to the poor ones would be small, as it was everywhere. But she had been sure that, with women so scarce, she could take her pick of the rich men and have an easy life the rest of her days.

But the rich men had been scarcer than she had expected and the women much more plentiful. Still, she had considered herself in real luck when Web Blaine had gravitated to her almost immediately. The son of the biggest and wealthiest rancher in the valley should make a fine catch.

She had liked Web from the start, but her goal of landing a rich husband had overshadowed any personal feeling. Then she had discovered that Web had broken away from Tree and was nothing more than a struggling homesteader. In fact, he was at odds with his father and was fighting Tree in order to hold his homestead.

Disillusioned, she had considered breaking with Web right then before any personal feelings built up to make the break difficult. But reason told her that blood was thicker than water—that the time might come when Eli Blaine would take Web back and Tree would fall into Web's hands. That was before she had discovered the stubbornness that ran deep in the Blaine blood.

She had played it carefully, making no commitments but keeping Web dangling, struggling to keep her own feelings under control. For her emotions were becoming a problem. She had to admit that, money or no money, Web Blaine was the prize catch of the valley. But she had set a rich husband as her goal and nothing, sentimental or otherwise, was going to veer her from her course.

Then her school term ran out, and logic said she should go back to her home in Omaha. It was then that Henry Farnsworth had made her a proposition. She had been aware of Farnsworth's interest in her for some time. But Henry Farnsworth was married, and so his interest had to be of a business nature, she thought. The storekeeper asked Valaree if she'd like to stay on in Bell and work at the store. She tried not to act too eager to accept the job.

Farnsworth became more and more confidential with his new bookkeeper until finally he offered her the job of taking care of more books, providing she could keep strictly confidential what she learned there. In exchange for this confidence and work, she would be cut in on a small share of the profits of the big organization that Farnsworth had going.

Valaree knew then that Farnsworth was a shrewd judge of character. Making a small fortune appealed to Valaree as no other inducement would have. So she had promised secrecy, and Farnsworth had given her the books of the Bell County Land Company. However, she found that she had two sets of books to keep. One set was for the inspection of both partners in the land company, Farnsworth and Eli Blaine. The other set was for Farnsworth himself. The figures there were entirely different from the ones in the other books. Eli Blaine had no part in the setup. It split things evenly between Farnsworth and Sim Dalbow.

There were two payrolls to keep up, too. One was for Eli Blaine to see. The other, from which the men were actually paid, showed big wages in some cases, blackmail in others. The blackmail kept certain men on the payroll, with absolute control of the men resting in the hands of Sim Dalbow.

This was the information that Web Blaine wanted. Valaree knew it, but she had resisted his efforts to get it from her. She had given her prom-

ise to Farnsworth, and it was with Farnsworth
that the possibility of riches lay.

In fact, the possibility was far greater than she
had at first anticipated. It had been only a month
ago that Farnsworth had let his true feelings be
known to her. He hadn't put things into so many
words; Farnsworth never did. But he had left her
with no doubt. Any time she said the word, Farnsworth would divorce his wife and marry Valaree.
Then she would have access to the fortune he
was building up.

Valaree wasn't especially proud of her achieve-
ment in snaring the affections of the fat man. But
it opened the door to the riches she had promised
herself when she had come here in the first place,
even though the prospect of marrying Farnsworth
repelled her.

Farnsworth hadn't objected to her seeing Web.
She had told him it was a good way to keep in
contact with the opposition, and he had agreed.

She tried to think back to the point where she
had begun to yield to the urge to tell Web everything she knew and depend on him to set things
right. Her thoughts settled on one minute, a
minute when she had looked through the restaurant window and had seen Web sitting at a table

talking earnestly with Darlene Bell. She didn't think Web was interested in Darlene, but how could she be sure? After all, she had been stalling Web for a long time. A man might get tired after so long.

She didn't like to think of herself as being jealous. Anyway, why should she be jealous of Darlene? Let her have Web. Valaree had something much better than Web. She had a share in the company that would soon control the entire county. And she could also have the big frog in the pond, Farnsworth, if she wanted him.

But in spite of all her reasoning, she couldn't squelch the feeling that Darlene was about to take something that belonged to her. And she resented it and wanted to fight for it, especially when that something was Web Blaine.

She thought of Henry Farnsworth, fat, bald, and altogether repulsive. But he had money, all the money Valaree could ever want. On the other hand, there was Web, everything she really wanted in a man, she admitted to herself now. But she'd have a struggle just making a living with him.

For a girl determined to head straight for her goal of a rich husband and a soft life, the choice seemed obvious. Why was it so hard to make?

After an hour of wrestling with the problem, she almost yielded again to the impulse to ride out and tell Web everything she knew about the land company. Her spirits soared at the thought. But they crashed down the next instant as she considered the consequences.

When Web learned the truth, he'd react quickly and violently. The result could very likely cost him his life. She couldn't stand that. And where would she be if she threw herself and her every hope at Web and he didn't survive the coming battle?

Not only that; would Web even listen to her now? He might give her the cold shoulder. He might not even believe what she told him unless she had the books to prove it.

Cold calm reason told her to sit tight and play the cards as they fell. She had a fortune at her fingertips. She'd be a fool to throw it all away. But cold reason was fighting a bitter battle with an emotion she had never encountered before. That emotion kept pounding at her, urging her to go to Web with everything she had, the information he wanted, her life and love, and to take her place beside him in the battle to come.

XI

It was a long ride home for Web. He still didn't know whether Valaree had had a hand in the raid the night before. Her anger at his accusations could have been merely a cover-up for her guilt, or it could have been righteous indignation. His blunt charges had been enough to make anyone strike back. And Valaree was not one to submit meekly to an insult. Web had to admit that was exactly what he had done—insulted her.

He scowled as he thought back on it. He had let his anger take control of his reason. He should have known he'd gain nothing that way—not from Valaree. Guilty or not, she'd strike back and he'd learn nothing. If he had ever had any chance of learning the truth from Valaree, it was gone now, killed by his own blundering.

Billy was back and stirring around the stove when Web rode into the yard. Web took care of his horse and went inside.

"Dinner ready?"

Billy spread his hands. "Can't find anything. Where do you hide your stuff?"

"Not much to hide," Web admitted. "Get your cattle over on Sitzman's place?"

"Sure," Billy said. "But I think I'll ride back up to my place this afternoon. I've got a feeling Tree will push some of its critters over on my land. They never wait long after a homesteader moves out."

Web nodded. "I know. I'll ride with you."

As the two left Web's place after dinner, Web was anticipating trouble when they reached Billy's homestead. Tree bordered Billy's farm, and it wouldn't take Dalbow long to get Tree cattle over there. He'd do it as quickly as possible and lay claim to the land for Tree.

Billy checked his gun as they rode. "I figure I might need this. What will you do if Eli is there?"

"Drive him off," Web said shortly. "He's got no more right there than any other claim jumper."

Before they reached the border of Billy's land, they saw Tree cattle spreading out from the boundary line dividing Tree and Billy's place. A hundred yards of the fence that Billy had built was flattened.

Billy slipped his rifle from its boot. "I'm going to kill me a skunk or two!" he yelled. "Coming?"

Web had to spur his horse to keep up with Billy. He could see only two men with the cattle. They had apparently pulled down the fence and were preparing to leave, letting the cattle move out in their own time.

Billy wasn't heading for the cattle but for the men who had just mounted their horses. Web, keeping pace with Billy, watched the men for the first sign of gun play. He recognized Sim Dalbow and, as they rode closer, he decided the other man was Ray Hickman, the man who had sided Jess Rakaw most of the time. Those two were both handy with guns, and Web doubted the wisdom of riding pell mell into a fight with them. But there was no stopping Billy. He was fired with a rage that only an exchange of bullets could placate. Web had to stay with him.

While still a hundred yards from Dalbow and Hickman, Billy pulled up his rifle and fired. Web was sure the bullet didn't come within twenty feet of the men.

Dalbow and Hickman returned the fire, their bullets coming much closer. They were mounted, but their horses were not running. Web brought up his own rifle. Billy had started it; now they'd both have to see it through.

But the two Tree men evidently had no stomach for a running battle with Billy and Web. After firing their one volley, they wheeled their horses and spurred them over the knoll in the direction of the Tree headquarters.

Billy didn't stop at the fence but rode through the big gap and pounded up the knoll in pursuit of the two men. Web didn't catch him till he reached the top. There he shouted at Billy and stopped him.

"If we chase them much farther, we'll run into the whole Tree crew," Web said. "Two was an even fight. It won't be if we catch them now."

"I didn't think Dalbow would run from a fight," Billy said. "The coward!"

Web hadn't expected that, either. Probably Dalbow was just waiting for a time when the odds would be more in his favor.

"We'd better get those Tree critters off your place," Web said.

They turned back through the gap in the fence

and rounded up the cattle that had been driven through. There weren't many, and Web and Billy drove them over the knoll and halfway to the Tree buildings before stopping.

They rode back and looked at the fence. "Can't do much with that today," Billy said with a sigh. "Reckon there's no point in fixing it at all as long as I'm living with you. I'll have to be right here to protect my fence. Anyway, we've got a meeting to go to tonight."

"Meeting?" Web said. "Where?"

"At John Niccum's. Guess I forgot to tell you. John was over to see you just before you got home from town. He said the homesteaders are pretty jumpy after what happened last night and want to get together and decide what to do. He figures you're going to have to talk pretty lively to keep them here."

"He's probably right," Web said with a sigh.

Web didn't realize how right until he and Billy arrived at Niccum's homestead that night shortly after dark. Niccum had two lanterns hanging in the yard and another in the barn where Web and Billy put their horses.

There were more homesteaders there than Web had expected. Several men from up on the dry land north of the creek were there. And there was one man there that Web hadn't expected at all. Fred Bell, the banker, had driven out in his buggy.

"John told me about the meeting," Fred Bell explained to Web, "and I figured I'd better come. After all, I'm involved in this deeper than many of the settlers."

Web nodded and moved to the end of the room where Niccum was waiting for him. Web had called the first of these meetings, and now they all seemed to expect him to go ahead with this one, even though he hadn't called it.

"I understand some of you are getting panicky," Web said. "Are you willing to give up your homes to a greedy land company?"

"Not willing," one man said. "But that isn't the problem. If we stay, we want some guarantee that we'll be able to keep our hides in one piece."

"Some of the boys have been threatened," Ed Ekhart said.

"So were you," Web said. "They burned your barn. But I haven't heard you saying you were going to leave."

"I'm not," Ekhart said flatly. "But not everybody is as determined to say here as I am."

"The land company is even moving up on the dry land, buying out farmers," Newt Prandall said. "If they make me an offer, they've got a deal."

Web remembered Newt Prandall from the last meeting. A little man, he had been the one who had been against organization of the homesteaders to fight the encroachments of the land company. Now he was ready to preach the wisdom of selling out to the company.

"They won't offer you anything," Web said disgustedly. "They know they can get your land for nothing. You won't fight. Anybody here had offers from the company?"

Hands went up over the room. Web looked at the men. All of them lived either on the creek or close to it.

"How about threats if you don't sell?"

Half of the hands that were up stayed up. These were men who had places right on the creek or immediately bordering Tree. One hand went up now, however, that hadn't been up when Web had asked about offers from the company to buy. That was Fred Bell.

"You've been threatened lately?" Web asked Bell.

Bell nodded. "They said a lot when I refused to sell them any more mortgages along the creek. But when they found out I meant what I said, they got nasty. Last night I found a note slipped under my door warning me to sell those mortgages, or else something terrible would happen to Darlene."

Web frowned as a murmur ran through the room. He hadn't expected them to follow up their first threat to harm Darlene. But maybe they would. Nobody would blame Fred Bell if he yielded to the pressure and gave up those creek mortgages if his daughter was in danger.

"They wouldn't dare touch Darlene," Ed Ekhart roared. "We'd skin them alive, and they know it."

Some men nodded in agreement; others only shook their heads. Web wasn't sure which side to take. The land company had already done things he hadn't thought possible in this day of growing law and order. It might not stop at harming a girl if, by doing it, the company could grab complete control of Dutchman Valley.

"I suppose they want the mortgages along the creek," Web said.

Bell nodded. "They want them the worst. But

they'll take any and all I have.

Web found a piece of paper and a pencil, spread the paper out on the table and did some rapid drawing.

"Come and look at this," Web said, holding up the paper. "It's not a very good drawing but it will show you what the land company is trying to do. Bell holds mortgages on all the creek land that Tree doesn't already have except Ekhart's, Billy McNeil's and mine. Isn't that right, Fred?"

The banker nodded.

Web pointed to the paper as the men crowded around. "If the company could get those mortgages, they'd foreclose in a week. Then they'd have the creek pretty well bottled up except for Billy McNeil to the west of Tree, Ed Ekhart down here, and me. They already have me completely surrounded."

"Are you going to pull out?" Prandall asked.

Web scowled at the little man. "You know the answer to that. I'm staying right there. Billy is staying with me, now that his place has been burned." Web looked over the other men. "Are you going to throw in the towel or hang and rattle?"

"I'm sticking," Ekhart said. "You know that."

"I'm not budging even if they get my mortgage," Ed Sitzman added.

Many of the other men nodded. Web wondered if they would stick. Here among the men who thought as they did, there was safety in numbers. How strong would their determination be in the fierce light of reality when they had to face the threats of the land company alone? For, no matter how they clung together, each man would be alone when he stood on his own land and tried to keep the company men off.

Web looked at the banker. "How about you, Fred? Going to hang onto your mortgages?"

Bell nodded. "If the men can stay on their land, I can hold the mortgages."

"Good." Web looked over the men. "Any questions? If any of you run into trouble, spread the word, and the rest of us will do what we can. As long as we stand pat, the land company won't be able to take over. But once they get the key places along the creek, they'll squeeze the rest of us out. We'll sink or swim together."

Web wasn't sure he had convinced any of the doubters when the meeting was over. He couldn't offer protection to any of them, because there was no way of telling where the land company gunmen would strike next. They could strike and be gone before help could arrive. The homesteaders realized that, and the ones with a shortage of courage would pack up and leave. Only the stouthearted would stay. Web wondered how many there were like that.

It was late and Web was tired when he and Billy got to bed. But it was a short night for them. Web was roused before daylight by someone hammering on his door.

Before putting his feet on the floor, Web reached over and got his gun. A killer would hardly hammer on the door to announce his presence, but Web couldn't afford to take even a small chance. The land company had proved how treacherous it could be.

Web stepped softly over to stand to one side of the door. "Who is it?" he demanded.

"Fred Bell."

Web hesitated only a moment. There was no mistaking Bell's voice although the banker seemed to be so excited he could scarcely talk.

Web threw open the door, his gun still in his hand. In the darkness, he made out the short form of the banker.

"Come in," Web said. "I'll get a light going.

What's wrong?"

"They kidnapped Darline," Bell said, clutching Web's arm. "You've got to get her back. It was your fault. You talked me into holding the mortgages back from them."

"Hold on!" Web said sharply. "Let's get this straight. How do you know Darlene has been kidnapped?"

"She's gone," Bell said. "And I found this note."

"Let me light the lamp," Web said, and pulled away from the hysterical banker. Hurrying to the table, he found the lamp and struck a match. As the light flared up, Web put the chimney back on the lamp and turned to look at Bell. His eyes were twice their normal size, and his face was several shades too white. In his hand he clutched a piece of paper. Web reached for it.

"What does it say?" Billy asked.

Web glanced at his partner. Billy had his pants and boots on and his gun in his hand. There was the same wildness in his eyes now that Web had seen yesterday when Billy had chased Dalbow and Hickman off his place.

Web read the note. "Sign over those mortgages to us before noon and nothing will happen to Darlene."

"They won't dare touch her!" Billy said.

"They've already done that," Bell said. "They kidnapped her."

"I'll cut their hearts out!" Billy shouted, almost as hysterical as Fred Bell.

"Now hold on," Web said sternly. "Let's reason this out. They want those mortgages. They say they won't harm Darlene if they get them."

"I'll sign them over," Bell said hastily.

"They might hurt Darlene, anyway," Billy said.

Web shook his head. "I don't think so. The people for miles around would band together and tar and feather them if they did. They won't run such a risk if they get what they want."

"Do you think they'll bring Darlene back if I sign those mortgages over to them?" Bell asked.

Web nodded. "Probably. But let's not go off half-cocked. They're giving you till noon. Let's use that time to try to find Darlene.

"But if we wait too long, they might kill her," Bell shouted.

"We won't wait too long," Web said. "If we can find Darlene and get her back safely, we'll have the upper hand. As long as the land company doesn't grab control of the valley, there'll be enough people here who will stand up to those gunmen once they find out they've stooped to kidnapping women."

"All I want is Darlene back safely," Bell said, calming down a bit. "I don't care what it costs me."

"Of course," Web said, nodding. "But we've got several hours till their deadline. Let's see what we can find out before you turn over that land."

It took ten more minutes for Web to bring Bell around to his way of thinking. And by that time, Billy had the horses ready for the ride to town.

As they left the yard, Web wondered if he had done right in getting the banker to delay yielding to the land company's demands. He had caused Fred Bell enough trouble already by talking him into defying the company and holding the key mortgages. Now if something happened to Darlene, it would be his fault again.

He'd have to see that it didn't happen. If he and Billy couldn't find Darlene soon, he'd let the banker turn the mortgages over to the company. When that happened, the homesteaders' battle for survival in Dutchman Valley would be lost.

XII

It was getting light in the east when Web and Billy rode into town with Fred Bell and reined up at Bell's house. Web didn't know what he would gain by going to Bell's to look around. But he had to start somewhere. He wasn't going to quit without a fight. And if he let Bell sign over those mortgages, the homesteaders' fight to stay in the valley would be over.

It was still half dark in Bell's house when they went inside. Mrs. Bell had the lamp lit and was moving around the house nervously.

"Did you send word to the sheriff at the county seat?" Web asked, wondering why he hadn't thought of that long ago.

Bell shook his head. "This is my problem. If I bring in the law, no telling what might happen to Darlene."

The ride to town had been a silent one, as Web had been deep in his own thoughts. But now there were questions that had to be answered.

"When did you find out Darlene was gone?" Web asked.

"A while after I got home from that meeting," Bell said. "I went to bed but I couldn't sleep. My wife had been to a church meeting. She got home before I did. But something woke her up, and she started nosing around. You know how nervous women are. She discovered that Darlene was gone and found the note."

"Did somebody sneak in here and take her right while you were in the house?" Billy asked.

Bell shook his head. "I think they kidnapped her while I was at that meeting at Niccum's and Harriet was at the church meeting. It's a wonder we even found out about it till this morning."

"If you found out just a while after you got home, it certainly took you long enough to get out to tell us," Web said.

"I wasn't sure what to do," Fred Bell admitted. "I'm not sure yet that I did the right thing. Maybe I should have kept quiet and done what they said."

"That does make sense, Web," Billy said.

Web shot a glance at Billy. Maybe Web was all wrong. Standing pat on his own hundred and sixty acres and defying the land company was one thing. Risking the property and now the lives of his friends and neighbors was another. He tried to tell himself it was for their own good. They were all fighting for their homes. But was it worth it to them? Would they rather surrender there and move somewhere else and try again?

"Do you want to quit, Billy?" he asked.

Billy frowned. "Of course not. But we can't let anything happen to Darlene, either."

Web nodded glumly, then turned to Mrs. Bell. "Did you find any clue as to who kidnapped Darlene or where they took her?"

Mrs. Bell shook her head. "I just found the note, that's all."

"Did she put up a fight?"

"No sign of it," Fred Bell said. Dawn was strong enough now to light the inside of the house without a lamp, and Bell led Web and Billy to Darlene's room. "You can see for yourself."

"Doesn't look like she had even gone to bed," Web said.

"Don't figure she had. Whoever took her must have come here before she went to bed and dragged her away."

"Did she take a coat and hat? It gets chilly at night."

"Didn't look," Bell said, and led the way to the coat closet in the hall. "Here's her hat. But her jacket is gone."

"Would she go without her hat?" Web asked.

Bell frowned. "Doesn't seem likely, since they must have let her get her jacket. Seems she would have taken her hat, too."

Mrs. Bell ran her hand along the row of jackets and hats. "Fred, her sunbonnet is gone."

"She's got a sunbonnet?" Billy asked. "I never saw her wear it."

"Few people did," Bell said. "Her aunt made it for her, but she didn't like it. She looked odd wearing it around town. Once in a while she would wear it when she worked in the garden. She preferred this Stetson when she went riding."

This seemed like idle talk to Web. Then suddenly it wasn't. Why would Darlene take her sunbonnet when she didn't like to wear it? She'd had a chance to get her Stetson when she got her jacket. Could it be that she was trying to leave a message by taking the bonnet instead of her hat?

"Why would she wear that bonnet?" Web

said thoughtfully.

"I don't know," Bell said. "When she wore it, she said she felt like she ought to be out on a farm slopping the hogs."

"That may be it!" Web said excitedly. "Maybe Darlene knew she was going to be taken to some empty farmhouse to be held till Fred signed over those mortgages. There are a dozen vacant farmhouses around town."

Bell's face brightened for a moment. "Could be. Darlene is a smart girl." Then his shoulders sagged. "But we haven't got time to check them all. Anyway, it might be too risky for Darlene. I'd better sign over those mortgages."

"Give Billy and me a while to look," Web urged. "We might find her. If we could beat them at their own game, it could turn things in our favor. Once the neutral people in town find out the land company is kidnapping women, they will surely side with us."

Bell sighed. "All right. I'll wait awhile. But if they put on the pressure, I'm going to sign to save Darlene."

Web motioned to Billy, and they went outside to the hitchrack. Before they mounted, however, Web pointed to a rider coming down the street in the uncertain light that immediately preceded the rising of the sun.

The rider came on and drew rein in front of Bell's house. Web had seen him once riding with Jube Altson, but he didn't know him.

"Something on your mind?" Web asked, watching the man closely.

"Just wanted to tell Bell to get ready to sign over those mortgages. I was told to remind him he didn't have much time."

"Who sent you?" Web asked.

The man sneered. "Wouldn't you like to know? Just tell Bell what I said."

"You tell whoever sent you that Bell will be in his bank office just before noon. Your boss can meet him there for the papers."

The man nodded and wheeled his horse. As he rode away, Bell came down the walk.

"Why didn't you let me talk to him?" he asked.

"Because you might have told him you'd sign right now," Web said. "Billy and I need a few hours to look. They said they wouldn't harm Darlene if you signed by noon. They won't if they're sure you will sign."

Bell sighed. "I hope you're right."

Web led the way out of town to the northeast. "There are a half dozen empty houses out here close to town," he told Billy. "They might feel so sure of Bell that they won't take her far."

But a check of the houses on that side of town turned up nothing. The sun was well up in the sky when they reined back toward town.

"Going back to Bell's to tell him to sign?" Billy asked eagerly.

Web shook his head. "I'm going to go to Farnsworth's store and talk to that pig. He might give us a clue. He's got a fat finger in this, you can be sure."

The store was open when Web and Billy reined up at the hitchrack. Inside the store, Web paused, looking for Jube Altson. If Altson was there, he'd have to tread lightly. If not, he could press Farnsworth hard enough so that he might tell something. He saw only Farnsworth rocking slowly in his chair behind the counter and Valaree down at the end of the counter, apparently engrossed in her books.

"What have you got to say about Darlene Bell being kidnapped?" Web demanded, moving up close to Farnsworth.

The fat storekeeper stopped rocking and stared

at Web, his eyes widening. "Darlene kidnapped? It's news to me."

Web knew it was an act. If Farnsworth hadn't planned it himself, he had certainly put his stamp of approval on it. Web glanced down the counter at Valaree. She had lost all interest in her books. She was staring at Web, shock and alarm in her face. This time, at least, Web thought, Valaree hadn't had anything to do with the land company's treachery.

"Has Darlene really been kidnapped?" Valaree asked, leaving her chair and coming down along the counter. "What for?"

"For ransom," Web said. "Fred Bell has to sign over the mortgages along the river before noon to keep anything from happening to Darlene."

"It can't be," Valaree said, shaking her head. "Nobody would stoop that low."

"The land company will," Web said grimly. "It has already done it."

"Valaree!" Farnsworth said sharply. "Get back to your books. This is a ghastly business. But the Bell County Land Company has nothing to do with it."

"Then how come the company is demanding

that Bell sign over those mortgages to save Darlene from harm?" Web demanded, shaking a finger in Farnsworth's face.

Farnsworth shrugged and pushed his rocker back. "I don't know anything about that," he said. "That's Bell's problem."

Web wheeled out of the store. Farnsworth wasn't going to tell him anything. But Web had learned something while he was in the store. Valaree had had nothing to do with this. Maybe she had helped plan the ambush of Billy and himself out at Billy's homestead. He wasn't certain about that. But he was certain about this. Valaree was shocked and horrified at Darlene's kidnapping. That had not been an act. Somehow Web got a lift out of knowing that.

"We'll head northwest," Web said to Billy when they were out of the store. "There are a lot of homesteads out there. We can't cover them all, but maybe we'll be lucky."

"Maybe she isn't at a homestead at all," Billy said.

"Maybe not. But that's the only clue we've got to go on."

Web led the way out of town, pushing his horse hard. There wasn't much time left. Even if they found Darlene, they'd have to get her free from her captors and back to town before Fred Bell had a chance to sign those mortgages over to the land company.

At one homestead where the farmer was still living, Web reined in.

"Did you see anybody go by here last night or this morning?" he asked.

The farmer shook his head. "I ain't seen nobody. And I ain't looking for nobody. Every rider that comes up, I figure he's one of the land company's hired gun slicks coming out to run me off."

Web nodded and nudged his horse on. It wasn't likely that anybody living there would have seen the kidnappers come by, even if they had come that way. They must have taken Darlene out of town last night, and nobody would have seen them in the dark. It was like looking for a needle in a haystack on a dark night, Web thought.

He fought off his depression and pushed ahead. He wouldn't give up till he had to. That would be soon enough.

"How many more places are we going to look?" Billy asked anxiously.

"We'll keep looking till we know it's too late to keep Bell from signing," Web said. "Do you want to quit?"

"Of course not," Billy said. "I want to find Darlene as bad or worse than you do."

"You don't act it sometimes."

"I've got different reasons," Billy said. "You just want to keep Bell from signing those papers. I want Darlene safe."

Web shot a glance at his partner. "So it's that way, is it?" he said, and let a grin creep across his face.

"I reckon," Billy said. Then he continued, alarm on his face, "But don't you dare tell anybody!"

"I won't have to," Web said, grinning. "One look at you—"

"Aw, shut up!" Billy grunted.

Web's grin faded from his face and he took out his watch. Less than two hours till Bell would be signing over those mortgages. At eleven, Web decided, he'd turn back to town. He wanted to be with Bell when he signed those papers. Something might come up at the last second. But it was too faint a hope to cling to.

Then suddenly, as their horses topped a knoll

overlooking the old Travis homestead, Web reined up sharply and motioned Billy back. Web had caught a movement down there where there shouldn't have been any.

"Travis has been gone for two months," Web said to Billy when they were back behind the knoll. "I saw something move down there."

Billy nodded excitedly. "Me, too. But I didn't have time to make sure what it was."

"May just have been a stray cow or horse. But let's not take any chances." Web thought hard for a moment. "There's a gully running along behind the barn down there. If we can circle and come up that gully, we should get close enough to find out if anybody is there."

"Let's go," Billy said, and reined his horse around.

It was half a mile around to a spot where they could drop down into the gully and not be seen by anyone watching from the house. They had to dismount and leave their horses ground-hitched. The gully wasn't deep enough to hide a horse.

Running, for time was becoming vitally important, Web led the way to the rear of the barn. Three horses were tied inside.

"No other reason why horses should be here,"

Web said. "And they're making sure they don't get out where they can be seen by anyone passing **by.**"

"How do we get to the house now?" Billy asked.

Web peeked around the corner of the barn. "Make a run for the back of the house. There's just one little window there, and they're not liable to be watching this way."

"We've got to surprise them," Billy said. "If we don't, they might harm Darlene or use her as a ticket to get away."

Web nodded. Billy was right. The kidnappers had to hold her only another hour and their mission would be accomplished.

Web led the way across the open area to the back of the house. As he crouched there, catching his breath, he thought that this might all be foolish. Those might not be Darlene's kidnappers in the soddy. But this was the end of the search as far as Web and Billy was concerned. If they didn't find Darlene there, they'd have no time to look farther.

Web motioned silently to Billy to go around one side of the soddy while he crept around the other. No words of warning were necessary.

Silently Web crawled around the corner. There was a bigger window there, but by staying low, Web crawled under it. He wasn't worried about any of the men being outside. Evidently one had been outside when he and Billy had first come in sight of the soddy, but they wouldn't be stirring around any more than absolutely necessary. They wanted to keep their presence there secret from all passers-by.

Then Web was at the front corner and peered cautiously around it. Billy was doing the same on the other side. Web lifted a hand, and both men leaped to their feet and sprang toward the door.

Web hit the door first and smashed it open, Billy just a step behind him. Two men were seated on boxes at a crude table. One reared backward, upsetting his box, but the other just sat there and stared. Over in the corner on the floor was Darlene. Her ankles and wrists were tied.

"Get their guns," Web said, holding his own gun on the two men.

"We ain't going to give you any trouble," the man still at the table whined.

"We're making sure of that," Web said as Billy collected their guns and tossed them over by the two rifles leaning against the wall.

Then Billy rushed over and untied the ropes holding Darlene.

"Toss those ropes over here," Web said, "and I'll wrap up these two buzzards."

"What are you going to do with them?" Billy asked.

"Leave them here and send the sheriff out for them. We haven't got time to drag them in now."

Billy tossed the ropes to Web, then turned his attention back to Darlene.

"I'm all right," Darlene assured him for the third time. "They were just holding me till Daddy signed over those mortgages."

"Let's get to town," Web said. "Maybe we can get there in time if we hurry."

As they collected the horses, leading the two extras, Web again looked at his watch. Time was running out. If Fred Bell was put under pressure, he wouldn't wait until noon to sign. If he didn't wait, all that Web and Billy had done that morning would have been wasted.

XIII

Their horses were lathered with sweat when they reined up in front of the bank.

"Let's get inside quick," Web said. "I've got a hunch that whoever shows up to get those mortgages for the land company won't wait till noon."

Inside the bank, Web surveyed things quickly. Henry Farnsworth was there, but he was at the cashier's window depositing some money. Fred Bell was in his office, nervously drumming his fingers on his desk, the door open as he watched people coming and going.

Bell came out of his chair like a cat springing at a mouse when he saw Darlene. With a cry, he ran out into the lobby of the bank. Web watched Farnsworth. He turned when Bell came out of his office, but his eyes widening a trifle were the only indication that anything unexpected was happening.

Web watched the reunion between father and daughter, but his attention stayed mostly on the pudgy storekeeper. He was willing to bet that Farnsworth had come there to get the mortgages from Bell. But he hadn't committed himself yet. Practically everyone knew that Farnsworth was one of the big wheels in the land company, but nobody had been able to produce proof of it. But if Farnsworth could have taken those mortgages from Bell, he'd have been in the driver's seat and he wouldn't have cared any longer about the false front he was putting up.

"Here on business, Farnsworth?" Web asked.

The storekeeper shrugged his shoulders and moved toward the door. "Just depositing some money."

But there was no mistaking the edge in his voice. Disappointment and rage were there, and even Farnsworth's rigid control of his emotions couldn't hide that fact.

Web turned to Bell when Farnsworth was gone. "Looks like we got here just in time."

Bell nodded. "I'd have signed hours ago if anybody had come and demanded it."

"Farnsworth would have done it if he'd been sure," Web said. "Evidently he felt certain no one would find Darlene and get her away from those two gun hands he had out there. Or else he didn't think you were running as scared as you were."

Bell scowled. "If it had been your daughter being held like that, you'd have sung a different tune."

"Maybe so," Web said.

"I'm getting out, anyway," Bell said. "They kidnapped Darlene once. They might do it again. Or they might do something worse. They won't quit."

Web frowned at Bell. "Just keep your shirt buttoned for a while. Billy and I nearly killed a couple of horses this morning trying to find Darlene in time to keep you from signing over those mortgages. We don't figure on having all that work wasted. They won't try anything else for a while. That's almost sure."

"How long?" Bell asked defiantly.

"Who knows?" Web snapped. He looked at

Darlene. "Can't you keep him caged up for a while so he can't give away those farms?"

"He'll be all right once he calms down," Darlene promised. "I think this has been harder on him than it has been on me. I'll take him home now. The bank can get along the rest of the day without him."

Web wasn't at all certain that Fred Bell would calm down. He'd had a terrific scare. He hadn't guessed that the land company would go to such lengths to get what it wanted when he had promised to hold back those mortgages. Web hadn't, either, for that matter. But it only raised the fighting blood in Web. It brought out the other side of Fred Bell.

Two other customers came into the bank, and immediately behind them Valaree stepped in. She didn't follow the other two to the cashier's window but turned directly to Wed.

"I want to talk to you, Web." She looked around. "Alone."

Web sensed the tension in her voice. "You name the place," he said.

In the back of his mind was the memory of the trap at Billy's place. But there was an intensity in Valaree's voice that wasn't to be denied.

"Come up to the store," she said softly. "Henry is gone."

"He was here a minute ago," Web said. "He may be back there by now."

She shook her head. "He went home for dinner."

Web went outside with Valaree and walked up the block to Farnsworth's store, Valaree at his side. Billy came to the door of the bank and watched them go. Web knew he was suspicious, and he was glad of it. Billy would stay on the alert.

Web, walking beside Valaree, tried to vanquish his suspicions. Until he had begun suspecting her of having a finger in the land company, his most pleasant moments had been when he was with Valaree. Now the pleasure was greatly diluted by his suspicions.

"Just what is so important that you can't tell me where people might hear?" he asked.

"When I tell you, you'll know," Valaree said, and led the way into the store.

As Valaree had said, Farnsworth was gone. In fact, the store was completely empty.

Web stopped and leaned against a counter. "We seem to be alone now."

Valaree looked around cautiously. "Somebody might come in. Let's go into the back room. We won't be interrupted there."

Suspicion tugged at Web. But there was an urgency in Valaree's voice that pulled him on. He had been sure for a long time that she had information he wanted, but he had nearly lost his life following wispy promises that he was going to get that information. This could be another of those traps. But this time Valaree was right with him. The promise was too close to ignore.

"Lead the way," he said.

As she went into the storeroom in the back of the building, Web followed. But he had his hand on his gun as he went through the partition door, his eyes probing the darkened corners, trying to see behind stacks of boxes.

"There's nobody here," Valaree said sharply as she stopped, watching him closely.

"There wasn't anyone over at Billy's place the other night when I got there, either."

"If you think I'm leading you into a trap, get out of here and stay out!" Valaree snapped, her voice rising sharply.

"I didn't say anything about a trap," Web said. "I'm just being careful."

The anger drained out of Valaree's face. "I can't blame you for that. You've got the whole country against you."

"What did you have to tell me?" Web asked, still tense and alert.

"How much do you know about the Bell County Land Company?"

Web moved to the one tiny window in the side of the storeroom and looked out through the dingy glass into the alley. "Not half as much as I suspect," he said.

Valaree nodded. "I can tell you everything about it. I keep books for it. Both sets."

"Both sets?" Web came over and sat on a box facing Valaree.

"That's what I said. On the surface, Henry Farnsworth and Eli Blaine are the two big wigs in the company. Eli wants to buy up every homestead he can to make a huge ranch. But he doesn't have the money, so he teamed up with Farnsworth, who does have the money. It's a partnership deal until Eli can pay back Henry Farnsworth with interest after they complete buying out the homesteaders. You are one of the big stumbling blocks."

Web nodded. "That I know. I'm sitting right in the middle of the land they're grabbing. But you said you had two sets of books.

Valaree stared at Web for a moment. "You're not going to like this. The Blaine-Farnsworth deal is handled in one set of books. The other books cover the business between Farnsworth and Sim Dalbow."

"Dalbow?" Web exclaimed. "Tree's foreman?"

Valaree nodded. "I don't keep those books out at my desk. They're kept in here. That's one reason I wanted to bring you here—to show you those books. They are the ones that really count. That's the real land company, but nobody knows it except a few of us."

"What does Dalbow have to do with it?" Web asked.

"Dalbow and Farnsworth made a deal. And it's the one that is going to stick. Farnsworth has no intention of sharing anything with Eli Blaine. He's putting up the money to cover the opera-

tions of the land company. Dalbow's job is to get
the men he needs to put the whole country under
gun law, if need be."

"He's about done it," Web said. "Most of the
men he's hired are on the dodge."

"I know that, too. Half of them are not paid
wages. They only get protection from the law. If
they kick over the traces, Dalbow or Farnsworth
will bring the law in on them. Some of them have
high prices on their heads. Jube Altson is one of
these. But they're loyal to the company, for they
have been promised a big pay-off when the settlers are gone and the company owns the whole
valley."

"If this deal is between Farnsworth and Dalbow, what about Eli.

"He's the front man now. As far as most people know, it is Eli Blaine who is gobbling up the
whole country. The land is being absorbed into
Tree as fast as the company gets control. The deal
between Farnsworth and Dalbow is for Dalbow
to furnish the gunmen, Farnsworth the money.
As soon as they get the land, Eli Blaine will be
eliminated some way. I've never heard them say
how they'll do it. That will be Dalbow's job, I

suppose. Dalbow is to get the Tree ranch and all the land south of the creek. Farnsworth is going to hold the farm land north of the creek for speculation. He thinks farmers will swarm in here in a few years. The dry years won't last. He figures to make a fortune then."

Web was silent for a minute after Valaree stopped talking. It all fitted into the picture he had been slowly putting together since he'd seen Eli Blaine the last time out at Tree. Eli was being used, and when they were through with him, they'd kill him.

Anger started building up in Web. He'd been fighting Eli for a long time now himself. But the thought of Farnsworth and Dalbow scheming against Eli brought out in Web a feeling of kinship for Eli, something he hadn't felt for years. Maybe it was just his hate of the Tree foreman and the fat storekeeper that overshadowed his anger at Eli. Or maybe it was his Blaine blood coming to the front to defend the name of Blaine.

"What made you decide to tell me this?" Web asked finally.

"I've been wanting to tell you for a long while, believe me." Her eyes dropped. "But Henry

Farnsworth trusted me. I don't break a trust lightly."

Web nodded. Maybe she hadn't broken the trust Farnsworth had put in her without a lot of thought. But how about the trust he'd put in her?

He was on the point of voicing his thoughts when he caught a movement at the tiny window. Instinctively he threw himself forward behind a stack of boxes.

A gun roared, glass shattered in the window and a bullet slapped into a wooden case. Valaree screamed.

Another bullet slammed into the packing case just above Web's head. He had his gun in his hand then, and he snapped a shot at the window, although he couldn't see anyone there.

Valaree was standing now, exposed to the marksman at the window. Web reached up and caught her arm, jerking her down beside him behind the stack of cases.

"Want to get killed?" he demanded.

"I don't know how they found out," she said, half sobbing.

"Maybe it wasn't hard," he said bitterly, thinking that once again he had been suckered into a trap.

"Nobody knew," Valaree said sharply, evidently realizing what he was thinking. "I made sure of that."

"Somebody sure found out," Web said.

"Jube Altson has been watching every move that I make," Valaree said. "But I was certain he had left town."

Web considered this for a moment. Was Valaree lying? Had she tried to give Altson and Farnsworth the slip when she came to him? Or had she deliberately led him in here? It was an airtight trap, all right. The only way out was the partition door through which they had come, unless there was a back door that he didn't know about. That partition door was right in plain view of the little window on the side. Web would never make it if he tried to reached that door.

A bullet again slammed into the packing case close to Web's hand. Valaree ducked as splinters flew. He frowned. This just didn't make sense. If Valaree had led him into a trap, why would they be shooting like this? Valaree stood as much chance of being hit as he did.

"I wish I had a gun, too," Valaree said,

twisting around to take a quick glance at the window.

"Stay down," Web ordered. "You wouldn't want to shoot at an old friend, would you?"

Valaree turned an angry glare on Web. "He's no friend of mine. If that's what you think, I don't care if they do kill you!"

Web was sorry he had said it as soon as the words were out. Whoever was doing the shooting was certainly not a very good friend of Valaree's. He snapped another shot at the window, but he had the futile feeling he was shooting at a shadow.

He looked at Valaree, staying flat on the floor now, her eyes filled with tears. Maybe they were tears of fright or maybe of anger. He felt his own anger fade away. He didn't doubt for an instant the truth of what she had told him about the land company and Farnsworth's double-cross of Eli. Why should he doubt Valaree's motive in bringing him there to tell him?

"I'm sorry, Valaree," he said softly, touching her arm. "Is there any other way out of here except through that partition door?"

Valaree shook her head. "There's a back door,

but it's locked from both the inside and outside. Farnsworth is afraid he'll be robbed."

Web nodded. That sounded like the fat store-keeper. He peered around the corner of a packing case, trying to find some way out of the trap. If Farnsworth came back to the store and added his gun to that of the ambusher, the odds against Web would be too heavy. On the other hand, if Web could hold out until Billy McNeil had time to get there and take a hand, the odds would swing the other way. For Billy would buy into the scrap, Web knew, unless some friend of the gun-man out there had made sure Billy didn't get down to the store.

Web snapped a shot at the window, and it seemed to touch off a barrage. It took Web a moment to realize that none of the bullets was slam-ming into the packing cases now. Billy McNeil had bought into the fight.

Web broke for the partition door, calling for Valaree to follow. He ran through the store and into the street, where the shooting had suddenly stopped. As he dashed around the corner to the north side of the store, he almost bumped into Billy coming back.

"That jasper can really run," Billy said, grinning. "You all right?"

Web nodded. "Who was it? Altson?"

"I think so. When I got here, I didn't stop long enough to see who it was. He must have thought an army was after him, for he didn't put up a fight. When he started running, he lit out so fast he didn't leave his name card. What did Valaree say?"

"Plenty," Web said. He turned to the girl, who was standing on the porch of the store. "You won't be safe here after what you told me." He hadn't really throught about Valaree's position before. She had put herself in real danger by coming to him with her story. "Will you be all right at your boarding house?"

Valaree nodded. "They won't bother me there."

"Stick close to your room," Web advised. "I'll be back as soon as I get some things straightened out."

As he rode out of town with Billy, he wondered when that would be. Things would happen now; the waiting period was over. As soon as Farnsworth and Dalbow found out from Jube Altson that their secret was out, they would move quickly.

XIV

Web found himself worrying more and more about Valaree as he and Billy got supper. Would Farnsworth rest easy until he had punished Valaree? Would she be safe even in her boarding house?

"What about those two kidnappers out at Travis' soddy?" Billy asked suddenly. "You didn't send word to the sheriff, did you?"

"I forgot about them," Web admitted. "It's too late to do anything now. Farnsworth or Dalbow or whoever sent them out there with Darlene must have let them loose before this."

Web considered riding back into town and finding some safer place for Valaree to stay. But there was no safer place unless he took her to Tree for his mother and Becky to protect. And he wasn't at all sure what kind of reception he'd receive there himself. Valaree, a traitor to the land company, certainly wouldn't be welcome.

But he'd have to go to Tree himself. He had to convince Eli that he was being used by Dalbow and Farnsworth. If he couldn't do that, all the information Valaree had given him would be of no use. Valaree would have risked her life for nothing.

Web suggested to Billy that they ride to Tree right at once, then discarded that idea himself.

"We'd likely be shot as prowlers," he said. "And there isn't a thing we could do tonight that we can't do better first thing in the morning."

But Web spent a restless night, the urge to be doing something crowding out sleep. An hour before sunup, he and Billy were mounted and riding toward Tree. It was growing light but the sun still hadn't appeared, when they rode through the orchard and into the yard. A light was on in the kitchen of the big house, where breakfast would be on the stove.

Web and Billy were not challenged as they strode up on the porch and Web knocked loudly on the door. A startled grunt sounded from the kitchen; then heavy footsteps came to the door. When the door opened, Eli was standing there, a rifle in his hand.

"What's on your mind?" he asked sourly as he looked at Web and Billy.

"Plenty," Web said, pushing past Eli into the room. Eli stepped back, and Billy came in, too. "Is Mom cooking brakfast?"

Eli nodded.

"Then sit down," Web said. "I've got some things to tell you."

Eli sat down reluctantly, the rifle across his lap. In blunt language, Web told him what Valaree had said about Sim Dalbow and Farnsworth using Eli to get control of the country and then planning to get rid of him.

Eli left his chair before Web had finished. He waved the rifle above his head like a whip and raved and swore.

"I might believe that of Farnsworth," he said after he had calmed down a bit, "but never of Sim Dalbow. Sim has been my foreman for fifteen years. He would never double-cross me!"

"I've got no reason to doubt what Valaree said," Web argued. "What would she have to gain?"

"I don't know," Eli stormed. "But Sim would never team up with that fat pig of a storekeeper. Why should he?"

"So he could own this whole south half of the valley," Web said. "Sim Dalbow is running from the law in Texas. He's got paper clippings in his stuff at the bunkhouse that says so."

"I don't believe it!" Eli said, stopping flat in his tracks.

"Did you ever look?"

"Of course not. I don't snoop into my men's pasts. Anyway, he keeps his things strictly to himself."

"Didn't you ever wonder why?"

Suspicion came into Eli's eyes for the first time. Slowly he sat down in his chair, watching Web closely.

"Was that what you were doing that day you killed Jess Rakaw?"

Web nodded. "I was snooping. Half of the men you've got here on Tree are on the dodge. Dalbow holds that over them to keep them under his thumb."

Realization of the truth crept across Eli's

face. His shoulders sagged, and he dropped the rifle beside the chair.

"I reckon I've known something was wrong for quite a spell," he said wearily. "But I didn't think Sim would cross me."

Heavy footsteps pounded across the porch, and the door burst open. "Who in—" Sim Dalbow stopped short, glaring at Web and Billy. "What are you two doing here?"

Eli didn't give Web or Billy a chance to answer. He came to his feet, stretching to his full height, and stepped over squarely in front of his foreman.

"Web tells me you and that pig, Farnsworth, are planning on taking over the land company as soon as you have all the valley under your thumb. And you figure on getting rid of me. What have you got to say to that?"

Dalbow rocked back on his heels as if from a physical blow. He stared at Eli for a moment, then drew himself up. "It's a lie, Eli. You ought to know that. Have I ever double-crossed you in anything? That's a lot better than Web can say for himself."

For a moment, Eli wavered. He looked from

his foreman to Web and back again. "Web says you're bringing in gun slicks to back up Farnsworth's play. You're to get Tree, and Farnsworth will get all the farm land north of the creek."

"Do you believe him?" Dalbow roared, stabbing a finger at Web. "Look how he crossed you in taking that homestead. He's keeping you from getting control of the valley. Now he's trying to split us, Eli. If he can do that, he figures he can whip us with those nesters he's got trailing him."

Web pushed forward as he saw Eli waver. "Back up those big words with something we can believe, Dalbow."

Dalbow frowned at Web. "You're not dragging me into a gun fight here," he said. "Not against two of you." He shot a glance at Billy.

"I'm not asking you to draw," Web said. "I just want you to tell the truth, if you know what that is."

"I told Eli the truth," Dalbow said, beginning to back toward the door. "You're hoodwinking him. If he can't see that, it's too bad."

Dalbow reached the door and backed out, turning swiftly and running toward the corral.

Web wheeled on Eli. "Well, which one do you

believe?"

Eli shook his head. "It's not like Sim to back off from a fight. He's got something else on his mind."

"He probably had planned to take over without risking a fight where he might get hurt or killed," Web suggested.

Eli nodded. "Maybe. I guess I've suspected Sim for quite a while, but I wouldn't admit it even to myself. Something's afoot today, all right."

Web tensed. "What do you mean by that?"

"An hour ago somebody rode in and went directly to the bunkhouse. I learned some time ago that I wasn't always welcome down there. But I went down this morning, anyway. By the time I got up and got dressed, though, the men were in the corral roping horses. They rode out toward town."

"You don't know what's up?"

Eli shook his head. "When I got down to the bunkhouse, nobody was there. Even Sim was gone. I thought he went to town with the rest."

"Maybe that's where he has gone," Billy said.

"I reckon," Eli said. "Probably Farnsworth has called the men in for that big raid he has been planning. It's to be a hit-and-run raid on some of the homesteaders who have refused to sell out. Maybe today is the day."

"They may figure they have to move before we can make use of what we've learned to unite the settlers against them," Web said.

"Let's get a move on ourselves," Eli said with some of his old drive.

Web's mind was spinning. "Maybe Farnsworth called the men in for a raid on the homesteaders. But I'll bet Dalbow went to town right now to change those plans. Part of their master plan is to get rid of you, Eli. Now that Dalbow knows you're wise to his scheme, he'll put that chore first."

"Do you think Dalbow will bring his men here to gun down Eli and you?" Billy asked.

Web nodded. "That's about it. We've got a real battle on our hands. But if we call the turn as to where and when we fight, we may catch them by surprise. Billy, you ride over to Sitzman's. Bring him on the double."

"Bring him here?" Billy asked as he started for the door.

Web shook his head. "Meet us at Ekart's.

We'll take the fight to them. We'll pick up John Niccum on the way."

Billy went out of the house on the run. Web turned back to Eli just as his sister, Becky, came into the room.

" I thought that was your voice, Web," Becky said. "What's wrong?"

Quickly Web told her, while Eli went to gather up some extra rifles.

"I'm glad you and Dad are on the same side again," Becky said. "I wish Gil was, too."

"Maybe he will be when he hears this."

Becky shook her head. "Gil has convinced himself that Farnsworth is going to be the kingpin in this valley, and he's stringing along with him. Gil never was a fighter, you know. But he tries to pick out the winning side and stay on it."

"We'll go by his place on the way to town," Web said. "Maybe he'll change his mind when we tell him how things are going."

Eli came back with two extra rifles. "May need them," he said. "This could get pretty hot."

Web picked up one of the rifles and hurried outside. It took a little while to catch and saddle a horse for Eli; then they pounded out of the yard and through the orchard.

Web led the way, riding past his own home-stead and crossing the creek toward Gil Harris' place. Becky was probably right—Gil would stick with Farnsworth, thinking he was going to emerge the kingpin. But Web had to give Gil the chance to join the Blaine forces. They'd need him. And even if they didn't need him, Web would give Gil the chance for Becky's sake.

"He ain't worth it," Eli said when he dis-covered where Web was heading. "Even if he rides with us, he won't fight. It ain't in him."

Web nodded. "You're probably right. But we have to do it—for Becky."

Eli nodded and said no more. There was no stir in the yard as the two riders reined up at Harris' hitchrack. Web frowned as he dis-mounted. Probably Gil had already gone to town with Dalbow's men, ready to ride in the raid on the homesteaders. He could think of no other reason for Gil being gone. He had very little work to do there since he had turned the place over to the land company.

"I'll check the house," Web said, and moved to the door. He knocked once, then pushed the door open. He stopped, staring in amazement.

Gil Harris was propped up in a chair facing the door. He had a gun in his hand, and his usual mild face was bruised and bleeding. His eyes were the eyes of a desperate man, forced into a corner, ready to kill.

"What happened here?" Web demanded, making no move to advance on the gun.

Gil Harris stared for a moment longer, then let the gun sag. "I got beat half to death," he said.

"Who did it?"

"Sim Dalbow. He came by here a few minutes ago, red hot to kill every living Blaine. He said I had to go with him. I told him I'd help the company but I wouldn't fight the Blaines. After all, they are my wife's family. He got mad and lit into me."

Web nodded. "You didn't fight back?"

"Sure I fought back. But you know I'm no match for Dalbow. Anyway, he was like a madman. I never saw him like that before." He gripped the gun hard. I'd like to get another crack at him. I'd kill him!"

"You'd better come with us," Web said.

"We're going to Ekhart's. Mrs. Ekhart can patch you up."

Harris nodded, got slowly to his feet and followed Web outside. Eli scowled when he saw Harris, and Web explained what had happened. The frown deepened on Eli's face, and he swore softly.

"Dalbow's gone crazy," he said. "We'll have to treat him like a mad dog."

At first Gil Harris had trouble staying in the saddle, but he gripped the horn with both hands and kept pace with Web and Eli.

"Where do you expect to find them?" Gil asked when the three stopped in the yard of John Niccum.

"I don't know," Web said. "We figure Dalbow went to town after his men to take them back to Tree and try to wipe the Blaines off the map. We're hoping to surprise them."

"Count me in," Harris said weakly, but with a savagery that Web had never heard in Gil Harris before.

"Strikes me that you've had your fight for today," Web said. "You're in no shape to get into a scrap like we're expecting."

Harris said no more, but slumped over the horn of his saddle while Niccum quickly saddled his horse and the four of them headed for Ekhart's.

In Ekhart's yard, Web helped Gil Harris off his horse and into the house. Gil was stronger than he had been back at his own place. Web supposed that the immediate effects of the beating were beginning to wear off. But still he looked unable to take a hand in another fight.

While John Niccum explained to Ekhart what Web had told him, Web took Harris into the house and asked Mrs. Ekhart to patch up his cuts and bruises as best she could. She shoved the tea-kettle onto the front of the stove and started bustling around, making bandages.

Web went back outside where Niccum and Ekhart were conferring in low tones. Eli stood to one side, trying not to notice the furtive looks of the two men.

"I suppose you're questioning Eli's right to be on our side," Web said, sizing up the situation at a glance.

Ekhart, always outspoken, nodded. "We sure are. We've been fighting Eli Blaine or his land company almost from the day we landed here. Now here he shows up, supposed to be on our side, just as we're ready to wade into a big fight. It doesn't add up, Web."

"Eli wanted the whole valley, all right," Web said. "But he made a mistake in the way he tried to get it. His foreman, Dalbow, and Farnsworth are in cahoots to double-cross him, take the whole valley, and do away with Eli in the process. He's got more reason to want to lick Dalbow and Farnsworth than we have."

Ekhart still shook his head. "If we lose to Dalbow and Farnsworth, we lose our places. But if we lick them, then Eli and Tree will take over."

"I just want to rid the earth of Farnsworth and that double-dealing foreman of mine," Eli said heavily. If we do that, I won't bother you. That I promise."

Ekhart nodded. Like everyone else in the country, he evidently knew that Eli's word was as good as his bond. "That's good enough for me," he said after a moment. "We can sure use another gun."

Billy rode in with Ivan Sitzman, their horses puffing hard.

"Dalbow come by yet?" Billy asked.

Ed Ekhart shook his head. "A hard-riding bunch went by here early this morning before daylight. And Dalbow himself rode by like his tail was on fire a while ago. But nobody has gone the other way."

"Do we wait for them here or go find them?" Niccum asked.

"Let's root them out," Eli said impatiently.

"No point in staging a battle here in Ekhart's yard," Web said. "Let's ride to town. They won't expect that. Maybe we can surprise them."

Gil Harris stood in the doorway, leaning against the jamb. "I'm coming, too," he said.

"You'd better stay here," Web said. "You're in no shape to ride, much less fight."

Harris frowned but made no move to come on out to his horse. Web made sure Harris' horse was tied securely to the hitchrack so he wouldn't follow the others, then mounted and motioned the men forward on the road to town.

XV

The six riders stayed on the south side of the river after leaving Ekhart's and approached the town from that side. Just before they topped the last knoll leading down to the bridge over Dutchman Creek, Web held up a hand and stopped the column.

"Let's go in fast and catch them off guard if we can," he suggested.

"What if they went out of town another way?" Ekhart asked.

"We'll have to chase them down. But I'm guessing they're still down there."

Web turned back toward town and kicked his horse into a gallop. If the gunmen were not in town, it would have to be because they had started on their raids before Dalbow got to town.

Web felt certain they hadn't, because either Ek
hart or Niccum should have been their first tar
get. The gunmen were probably changing thei
plans to hit Tree first and kill Eli and Web.

The town looked as peaceful as usual when th
six riders came in sight of it. The only movemen
on the street was at the livery barn just beyon
the bridge. Web spurred his horse down th
road toward the bridge. If Dalbow's men sav
them coming, the battle could start at any min
ute. If the gunmen were taken by surprise, the
would probably hole up in Farnsworth's store

Web was within fifty yards of the bridge wher
the first volley of shots ripped across the cree
from the livery barn. He didn't rein up bu
waved his hand forward toward the creek. Veer
ing his horse off the road, he spurred him ove
the bank of the creek as another volley of shot
roared from the barn.

Throwing himself from the saddle, Wel
slapped his horse on the hip, sending him up th
creek while he ran to the north bank an
dropped down out of sight of the men in th
barn.

The other five horses poured down the cree

bank, and the men dived from their saddles. Web made a quick inspection. Only Ed Ekhart had a wound, and it wasn't too serious; just a groove cut in his arm.

"I lack a lot of being dead," Ekhart said grimly. "They're going to find that out in a minute."

"We were mighty lucky," Web said. "If they'd waited till we were closer for that first volley, half of us might be dead. They can't see us now, but we can't see them, either."

He leaned up against the steep bank and peered over at the barn. The others did the same. Eli, impatient, ripped a shot into the barn.

Just as his bullet plowed into the split log side of the barn, a man broke into the clear to the left, apparently headed for some trees that grew along the bank of the creek upstream from the barn. The instant the shot roared from Eli's gun, the man dug in his heels and wheeled back toward the barn. A shot from a gun beside Web cut him down there.

"Thought they'd flank us and get us in a crossfire, I reckon," Sitzman said. "Guess we nipped that in the bud."

For five minutes bullets crossed the short space between the barn and the river bank like hailstones in a bad storm. But Web was certain it was just wasted ammunition. Nobody was exposing himself.

"This could go on for a long while unless somebody runs out of ammunition," Web said to Billy as he reloaded. "It will be a lucky shot that hits anything."

"We're not liable to run out of ammunition right away," Billy said. "We came to fight."

A yell from the barn was proof that someone had scored a lucky hit. After another minute of rapid fire, the barn became quiet. Web held up a hand, and the firing from the river bank stopped.

"Figure it's a trap?" Niccum asked.

Web peered over the bank and caught a glimpse of a man running on the far side of the barn.

"Looks like they're backing off to the feed store," he said. "They can hole up there safely enough and then pick us off if we try to come after them."

"What are we going to do?" Eli said, looking over the bank. "We can't let them get away."

"Let's take over the barn," Web said.

Without waiting for the others to agree, Web scrambled up the creek bank and dashed for the barn. There might be a man or two staying in the barn waiting for just such a move, but it was a chance Web had to take.

No shots came from the barn, and all six of the men reached the rear of the building safely. Web shoved open a sliding door, and they all hurried inside.

All around were signs of the battle. Empty cartridge cases were in piles where men had been firing through cracks and knotholes. The man who had made a futile try at reaching the trees was still lying just outside the barn where he had fallen. Blood splattered the hay where the wounded man had been standing when he'd been hit. But the man was gone, evidently still able to retreat with the others.

"They'll be harder to roust out of that feed store than they were here," Sitzman said.

"Wish I had this arm fixed," Ekhart grumbled. "It's starting to hurt like blazes."

Web looked at the arm. "There's a doc not far away, but I'm afraid we'll have to clear the road a little before we can get to him. Anybody know how to put on a bandage?"

"I'll wrap it up," Niccum said. "But I'm no doc."

It soon became evident that it was another stand-off. The feed store offered Dalbow's men better protection than the barn had, but Web's men, carefully choosing their protection, were also fairly secure from probing bullets.

"How many men does Dalbow have?" Sitzman asked. "Can anybody make a guess?"

"I can," Eli said. "He must have all the Tree hands, plus Jube Altson. That would give him about nine to start with. We got rid of one out there." He jerked a thumb toward the outside of the barn. "And we sure crippled another one. So that would leave about seven able-bodied men. But some of them are real handy with a gun."

"Dalbow is a gun fighter and so is Altson," Web said. "Maybe Ray Hickman, too."

Eli nodded. "There are a couple more in Dalbow's outfit who know which end of a gun bites. We can't afford to take any chances."

The door of the barn slid open and Web

wheeled, his gun cocked. But he let it sag as he saw Gil Harris come in, a bandage around his head and patches on his face.

"I thought we left you at Ekhart's," Web said.

"You left me. But you couldn't make me stay there. I've got a score to settle with Sim Dalbow."

"You're in no shape to take a hand in this fight," Eli said.

"I sure ain't staying out of it," Harris retorted. "Where are they?"

"In the feed store. About all we can do is take pot shots and hope we might be lucky."

"Dalbow with them?"

"I reckon," Web said. "He's the one who holds the whip hand over a lot of those men. If it wasn't for what he knows about them, they could be drawing a lot better wages than they are from the land company."

Another ten minutes slipped by with no advantage gained by either side. Web began to grow uneasy. Dalbow would think of some way to get at the men in the barn soon. Web looked at the men around him. Gil Harris had no business being there, and Ed Ekhart should have been home where his wife could dress his wound.

"You'd better go back to Ekhart's, Gil," he said. "And take Ed with you. He needs that arm taken care of."

Harris looked at Ekhart and nodded. But Ekhart objected.

"If you think I'm pulling out of this thing before it's over, you're crazy," he said. "I can still use my other hand, and it's the one with the gun in it."

Web turned his attention back to the fight. Behind him, he heard the sliding door open again and turned to see Gil Harris slipping outside. Apparently Gil's injuries were overcoming his craving for revenge, and he was going back to Ekhart's.

Web was glad that Gil had pulled out of the fight. But the fight itself was a stalemate now. Web concentrated on the one side window of the feed store facing the barn, from which shots had been coming at irregular intervals. In the next few minutes he fired twice as a head appeared for a second at the window. But he was sure he had missed the elusive target both times.

Then suddenly his attention was caught by a movement off to the left of the feed store. There

was no window on that side of the store, but there
was a small back door.

Web wheeled to the other men in the barn as
soon as he recognized the figure stealing up to
the feed store.

"Gil's out there, coming up to the back door
of the feed store," he said as the men stopped
shooting and looked at him.

"He'll get himself killed for sure," Sitzman
said.

"We can't stop him or bring him back," Web
said. "Let's give him the best protection we can.
Keep those men up there busy looking our way."

Web turned back and slammed a shot into the
feed store. Other guns sent a barrage of bullets
toward the barricaded gunmen.

Web didn't pay much attention to where his
shots were going. He was keeping one eye on
Gil Harris. He certainly hadn't expected such an
act of his brother-in-law. Harris must have gone
upstream a couple of hundred yards under the
protection of the creek bank before climbing out
and beginning his circle to bring himself up on
the blind side of the feed store.

Now he was within striking distance of Dalbow's men in the store. But the only way he could get at them would be to open that door. When he did, he'd meet a hail of bullets. It was an insane move, the way Web saw it. But Gil Harris had been bordering on the insane ever since he'd taken that beating from Sim Dalbow. That beating had released something in Harris that Web hadn't realized was there.

Harris moved up to the back door of the feed store and paused to catch his breath, glaring at the door, his gun held in rigid fingers.

"When he kicks open that door, it will be his last move," Sitzman said softly at Web's elbow.

"Let's keep their attention until he does," Web said. "Give him every possible chance to do what he wants to do."

Web and every other man in the barn knew that Harris had just one thing in mind—to kill Sim Dalbow. The fact that he was sure to get killed himself didn't seem to matter to him.

Web, his gun freshly reloaded, emptied it into the feed store as he saw Harris draw back to kick the door. Guns on either side of Web sent all their fire power at the little store.

Then Harris had kicked the door open, and the guns up at the feed store were suddenly silent. There were two shots in the sudden stillness; then a crescendo of reports rocked the little feed store.

Web, watching the rear door where Gil Harris had disappeared, saw him come out now, reeling wildly. Ten feet from the door he collapsed, and the way he fell left no doubt in Web's mind that he would never get up again.

Web turned his eyes back to the feed store itself. Draped across the window through which much of the shooting had come was Sim Dalbow. His hat was gone, and it looked from that distance as if half his head was gone with it. Harris had accomplished his mission at the cost of his life.

"Well, he got him," Ivan Sitzman breathed. In the stillness that gripped the barn and the street after the barrage of shots, the words sounded like a shout.

Eli Blaine's voice was husky when he spoke. "That's the first thing Gil Harris ever did that I was proud of. Let's not let it be wasted."

Eli broke the stillness with a shot at the feed

store. In a moment the other guns in the barn had joined in. A few spasmodic shots came back, but there was none of the concentration of fire that had marked the battle before Harris' interruption.

"I think they've had enough," Billy said. "Dalbow was their leader. With him gone, they don't have anything to fight for."

Web nodded. The men who had feared Dalbow's threat to turn them in to the law if they failed to do his bidding were free from that threat now. The others, hired with a promise of good pay from Dalbow when he and Farnsworth took over the valley, might have doubts that Farnsworth would live up to Dalbow's promises even if they won.

Web kept up his firing. If there were doubts among the men in the feed store, more bullets pouring through the window would do nothing to ease those doubts.

Suddenly, through the rear door which was still open, a man leaped and wheeled to put the building between himself and the livery barn. Web couldn't see who it was, and he had made his move so quickly that not a shot was fired at him.

"Looks like they're going to make a run for it," Sitzman said. "The next one who tries going through that back door is going to get surprised."

But nobody else tried breaking through the doorway. After a long lull in which no shots were fired from the feed store, a gun came through the window to spin and settle in the dust. Then another gun and a third followed it.

Web held up his hand, and the firing in the barn stopped. "Let's see what's on their minds now."

"We're coming out," a voice shouted when the guns had stopped, "without our guns."

"Let's see you," Web shouted back.

The front door of the feed store opened slowly, and men started coming out, hands high. Four seemed to be unhurt, and they were followed by two who couldn't hold their hands up. One, Web guessed, was the man who had been hurt in the barn. The other must have been wounded by a shot from the barn or by Harris when he burst into the feed store.

Web led the way outside and up the street to the men. Billy and Ivan Sitzman turned to

Web.

"Reckon that's the end of the land company."

"There's one man missing," Eli said. "Tree had eight men. Two are dead, and here are the other six. Where's Jube Altson?"

"He's gone," one of the men said.

Web remembered the man who had run just before these men had surrendered. The fight wouldn't be over until Jube Altson was dead or disarmed. Web checked the loads in his gun. He still had a battle to fight.

XVI

Web stopped at the feed store to look down the street. Billy caught up with him there.

"This is my fight, too," Billy said. "You take one side of the street. I'll take the other."

Web thought for a moment. Billy was a farmer. A gun didn't fit in his hand as it did in Web's. This wasn't Billy's kind of fight.

"Check the barn at Reilly's," he said. "Alston stays at Reilly's. He probably keeps his horse there, too. He might try to make a run for it."

"If he does, shall I let him go?"

Web nodded. "Don't try to stop him. If he gets out of the country, that's good enough. I'll check at Farnsworth's. If you find that Altson has skipped out, come and tell me."

"And if I find he hasn't skipped out and I can't locate him at Reilly's, I'll be along to help you," Billy said, and turned up the street toward Reilly's Boarding House.

Web turned his attention back to Farnsworth's. He had no illusions. Jube Altson had run from the feed store. But he wasn't the kind who would quit. He had probably left the store because the men there were talking surrender, and Jube Altson wanted no part of that.

Web could only guess what arrangements Henry Farnsworth had made with his personal bodyguard. But knowing men like Altson, he felt sure that Altson had demanded a big price for making sure nothing happened to Farnsworth until the valley fell into the land company's hands. Jube Altson wouldn't leave town now without the money he thought he had coming.

Web dodged up the street to the bank and stopped there. There was a good chance that Altson would expect someone to tail him, and he might wait to cut Web down before having his showdown with Farnsworth. But there was no sign of the gunman anywhere along the street.

Web moved cautiously on to the barber shop

and the harness shop. Then he was faced with Farnsworth's big store. It was the biggest building in town, with the exception of the livery stable. Web tried to guess where Altson would be. But it was useless. Altson could be wrangling with Farnsworth right now. Or he could have gotten what he wanted from the fat storekeeper and already be gone. Or he could be just waiting for someone like Web to show up so he could earn more of Farnsworth's money. Web was willing to bet that Farnsworth had put a good price on his head.

Web circled to the back of the harness shop and made his break from there. He crossed the alley to Farnsworth's store in a swift zigzagging run. Nothing happened, and he began to consider his next move. He'd have to go through the front door of the store. There was no other way in.

Web cocked his gun and charged around the corner of the store and through the front door. His gun swept the inside of the building, looking for the trouble he'd been sure he'd find there. But his appearance was greeted by a complete, unnatural silence.

For a long while, Web crouched just to one side of the door and studied everything in sight. Henry Farnsworth was seated in his rocker, slowly weaving back and forth. He barely looked up as Web came in. Farther back, Valaree sat at her desk, working on her books. But she didn't look up, either.

Tension pulled a tight knot in Web's stomach. Why was Valaree there? He'd told her to stay at her boarding house. After yesterday, Farnsworth would hardly call her back to work unless there was a good reason. And why was she ignoring him now? Wasn't she concerned about what happened to him?

Suddenly he knew the answer. Jube Altson was there. If Farnsworth and Valaree had both shouted it, he wouldn't have been any more certain.

He scanned every box and barrel in the big room. There was no sign of Altson. If he was in this main room, he surely would have opened fire already, Web decided. Web thought of the back room where Valaree had talked to him yesterday. Altson could be waiting there in the semi-darkness. The second the door opened, he would be able to riddle a man with bullets before the victim could get inside or even see who was in there.

Web jerked the muzzle of his gun toward Farnsworth. "Get out of that chair, Farnsworth."

The rocker stopped. "What for?"

"Because I said so," Web snapped. "Come on, or I'll see how far a bullet will go through all that tallow."

With surprising speed, Farnsworth got out of the rocker and moved into the center aisle of the store. "Now what do you want?"

"I want you to go with me to that back room. You're going to open the door and go in first."

For a second Farnsworth glared at Web, both fear and cunning in his eyes. Finally, without a word, the storekeeper began to shuffle slowly toward the back door. Then he stopped five feet short of the door.

"If you want to go in there, you can go yourself," he said.

The fat man stepped to one side, and Web jabbed the gun in his ribs.

"You go first, I said."

"You're the one who wants to go in there; not me."

There was a whine in the storekeeper's voice. Web had expected that. He shot a glance across at Valaree, who was straight across from him now. Her eyes were wide, and he read the unveiled fear in them. Was it fear for the storekeeper? If Altson was in the storeroom, he'd shoot the first thing he saw appear in that doorway. That was going to be Farnsworth.

Web prodded Farnsworth closer to the door, but he couldn't keep his eyes off Valaree. Her eyes flicked to one side, then darted back at him. A chill ran over him. Did she mean something by that?

"I'm not going in there," Farnsworth said defiantly.

There was no fear in the storekeeper's voice now. Something was wrong. Web could feel it, but he couldn't quite put his finger on it.

"Hold still!" he snapped as Farnsworth began shifting to one side.

Even as he said it, Valaree screamed, the sound cutting through Web like a knife. "Over here, Web!"

Web wheeled, knowing in that instant what he was going to see. Jube Altson was coming up out of a crouch from behind the counter next to Valaree's chair. Even as he brought his gun forward, Valaree struck at his gun arm.

The gun discharged, the bullet slamming into a counter on the far side of the store. The gun itself clattered to the counter in front of Altson and slid to the floor on the other side.

But Web had no chance to take advantage of the situation. Farnsworth threw himself at Web. The fat storekeeper was soft, but he carried a lot of weight, and Web was knocked off balance. He reeled back against the counter across from the spot where Valaree was struggling with Altson.

Web managed to hang onto his gun and brought it around with all the force he had, hitting Farnsworth in the stomach. The breath exploded out of the big man, and he doubled over. Web arched the gun down on the fat's man head, and Farnsworth slumped forward with a long sigh.

Web wheeled his attention to Altson across the room. The gunman, unable to reach his gun, had grabbed Valaree around the waist and had pulled her out from behind the counter. He was holding her as a shield while he struggled forward, trying to reach his gun. Web couldn't shoot.

Valaree was putting up a terrific struggle, and Web admired her for it. He leaped over the big body of the storekeeper that had him trapped against the counter and started toward the two.

But just as he cleared the fat man on the floor, Altson lunged forward, getting his hands on the gun. He dragged Valaree down with him, and Web still didn't dare risk a shot.

Then Valaree, seeing that Altson had the gun, lunged the other way, leaving the back of her dress in Altson's hand. But his other hand held the gun, and there was murder in his eyes.

Web dived to the floor, firing as he fell. He heard Altson's gun roar and felt a tug at his shirt as he hit the floor. He rolled over and brought his gun up again. Twice more he squeezed the trigger as rapidly as he could. Altson's gun roared once more, the bullet slamming into the floor halfway between him and Web. Then he collapsed, his gun hand doubled under him.

Web came to his feet, running to Valaree where she had fallen when her dress had given way.

"Are you hurt, Valaree?"

She shook her head as she got to her feet. "Nothing but a scratch or two. How about you? Are you hit?"

"Just a nick in the side," he said. He showed her his shirt where Altson's bullet had torn it as it passed. "Looks like we'll both need some new clothes."

"I was afraid we'd need shrouds," Valaree said.

Billy McNeil came running in. He took one look and turned to the door. "Come on down here," he shouted into the street. "Web's got it all finished."

Farnsworth groaned and sat up. Web pulled him to his feet and helped him to his rocker just as Eli and Sitzman came in.

"Looks like you finished things up about right, son," Eli said. "John took Ed to the doc. Maybe this fat pig could use a doc, too."

"This should put an end to the land company," Billy said. "But we've still got Tree to live with." He looked sharply at Eli.

Eli shook his head. "You just helped get me out of a tight spot. I reckon I owe you farmers something besides a peck of trouble."

"We had a deal, Eli," Farnsworth said, leaning forward in his chair. "Jube told me Sim Dalbow is dead. But that doesn't end our agreement. We'll still own this entire valley."

"You'll be lucky if you get out of this town owning the shirt on your back," Eli said. "I'll admit I was as big a hog as you for a while. But I'm through grabbing. In fact, I'm turning Tree over to Web and Becky, if they'll have it. You take your filthy money and get out of the country."

"I own two dozens farms north of the river," Farnsworth roared. "Nobody is going to run me out without paying me for them."

Ivan Sitzman moved up in front of the storekeeper. "You ran out a lot of my good friends and neighbors. Now I'll consider it a real pleasure to return the favor."

"You sodbuster!" Farnsworth yelled. "You can't run—"

The fat man's voice dwindled and died as he

stared into the steady cold blue eyes of the homesteader.

"Want to bet on that?" Sitzman asked softly.

Farnsworth sank back into his rocker, a beaten man. Web watched the men gather around Farnsworth. Farnsworth would be lucky to get out of town alive.

But Web had more interesting things than Farnsworth to think about. He caught Valaree's hand and pulled her toward the storeroom in the back of the building.

Valaree glanced back at the men outside as Web was closing the door. "They'll talk," she said softly.

"I hope they do," Web said. "I expect all of them but Farnsworth to be at our wedding."

She dropped her head. "You haven't asked me yet."

"I'm asking now."

"You know the answer." She looked up then. "I made a terrible mess of things, Web. It took me a long while to get up enough nerve to try to straighten them out. I've never been so scared as I was today when Jube Altson came to the boarding house and made me come here and pretend to work so he could lure you into a trap. I tried to warn you."

"You did a good job," Web said. "According to what Eli said, we'll have Tree to live on and—"

"I wouldn't care if you didn't even have a homestead to live on, Web. I know now what I want. And it isn't a ranch or money or anything but just you."

He kissed her then, and it didn't matter a bit to him that Billy opened the partition door just at that moment to look for him. Web wanted everybody to know.

"You're going to have a hard time ever losing me now," he said softly in Valaree's ear.

☐ **YES!**

Sign me up for the Leisure Western Book Club and send my FREE BOOKS! If I choose to stay in the club, I will pay only $14.00* each month, a savings of $9.96!

NAME: _____

ADDRESS: _____

TELEPHONE: _____

EMAIL: _____

☐ I want to pay by credit card.

☐ **VISA**   ☐ **MasterCard.**   ☐ **DISCOVER**

ACCOUNT #: _____

EXPIRATION DATE: _____

SIGNATURE: _____